MOONLIGHT AND SHADOW

When Andrew Melbury impulsively marries Leah Hancock, his grandmother's companion, he is aware they barely know each other. But all such considerations seem irrelevant in the face of their love. It is only after a potentially fatal encounter on a moonlit road in Sherwood Forest that Andrew begins to question why Leah has always been so reticent about her past. What secrets has she been keeping from him? And are both their lives in danger?

Books by Jasmina Svenne
in the Linford Romance Library:

AGAINST ALL ODDS
THE RECLUSE OF
LONGWOOD PRIORY

JASMINA SVENNE

MOONLIGHT AND SHADOW

Complete and Unabridged

LINFORD
Leicester

First published in Great Britain in 2008

First Linford Edition
published 2009

British Library CIP Data

Svenne, Jasmina M.
  Moonlight and shadow- -
  (Linford romance library)
  1. Secrecy- -Fiction. 2. Love stories.
  3. Large type books.
  I. Title II. Series
  823.9'2–dc22

  ISBN 978–1–84782–796–8

Published by
F. A. Thorpe (Publishing)
Anstey, Leicestershire

Set by Words & Graphics Ltd.
Anstey, Leicestershire
Printed and bound in Great Britain by
T. J. International Ltd., Padstow, Cornwall

This book is printed on acid-free paper

1

For a long time now only the drumming of hooves and the creak of wheels had punctuated the silence. Andrew could not help stealing a glance at Leah. But although the moon was just past the full, the dense canopy of Sherwood Forest allowed only fitful glimmers to penetrate the interior of the coach.

He traced a gleam of moonlight along Leah's cheek with his finger, unable to believe that she was truly his. They had only been married three days and his head was still reeling.

'Cold, darling?' he asked, feeling her shiver.

'A little.'

'Come here. I'll soon warm you up.'

She snuggled against his breast.

Andrew slipped his hand into her velvet muff — the most recent of the gifts he had showered on her, despite her protests — so he could clasp her fingers. But he could sense that all was not well.

'You're not still fretting about tomorrow?' he asked, squeezing her hand.

She returned the playful pressure. 'I hope Papa will agree to see us. Now we are so close, I almost wish we had decided to stay the night in Nottingham. And yet if we had done so, I don't think I could have borne the delay.'

'Can a clergyman be so unforgiving?' he asked.

'I don't know. I've never angered him so much before. At first I hoped he would forgive me within a month or two of my departure, but . . . ' She shrugged.

'Well, we'll do what we can to appease him, but if he proves unreasonable, we won't let him spoil our marriage, will we?' Andrew tried to sound encouraging. The sole purpose of their journey so soon after their wedding was to try to forge a reconciliation between Leah and her father.

'I promise,' she said, twining her arm around his neck. 'Don't worry. Papa ought to approve of you, even if he doesn't approve of me.'

Andrew hoped she was right. He was rich enough to satisfy most parents, as long as he did not set his sights on the daughter of an aristocrat, but he feared the suddenness of their wedding might give a false impression of his character. He had always considered himself a rational man, not so mad as to marry on the strength of a month's acquaintance. And yet that was precisely what he had done.

'And do you approve of me?' he asked, trying to lighten the mood.

'Not in the slightest.'

'But you are in love with me?'

'Whatever gave you that idea?' He could hear warm laughter gurgling in her throat.

'Then why did you marry me?'

'For your money, of course.'

'And is there nothing that could change your mind, you shameless fortune hunter?' he asked, smiling through the darkness as she tilted her face towards his.

'Nothing that I can think of.'

'Not even this?'

He leaned closer to kiss her. The carriage rocked violently as it encountered a pothole, jolting them apart. Leah started giggling as she nestled against him and he found his thoughts drifting backwards.

★ ★ ★

Andrew drew rein and fanned himself with his tricorn. It was unseasonably warm for September. He had had a dusty ride, though he set out at an early hour from the inn in Hereford, hoping to reach his destination before the heat became unbearable. There was barely a mile to go, but the glint of the river through the trees was too tempting. He dismounted, but before he could reach

4

the water's edge, something fluttering further downstream caught his eye.

A dip in the ground had created a small waterfall, no more than a foot or two in height. There, balanced precariously on the flattened boulders, white toes curled to retain her footing, was a girl.

She was bent dangerously forwards, reaching for something in the water. Her full petticoats and gown were gathered over one arm, allowing him an illicit glimpse of neat ankles and calves.

Andrew tethered his horse in the shade. Lush grass whispered against his boots as he strode towards the waterfall. He dared not call out, afraid of startling the girl and making her lose her balance. Her back was towards him and he guessed her absorption in her task and the chuckling of the water prevented her from hearing his approach.

He noticed a pair of black leather shoes with metal buckles in the grass next to a tree stump. Beside them lay a pair of white stockings with colourful clocks embroidered on the ankles, dropped in an intertwining tangle with a pair of garters.

Andrew wrenched his gaze away. As he came within hailing distance, the stranger straightened up and he could see she was grasping the brim of a straw hat from which drenched ribbons trailed like the hair of a mermaid.

'Oh,' she gasped, catching sight of him.

He barely had time to register her flush. At the same moment she missed her footing and fell.

Without pausing to think, Andrew plunged into the river. It was not deep, nor was the current particularly strong, but the coldness of the water came as a shock. The girl had fallen on her side, one arm flailing, trying to find something to cling to. Andrew clasped her wrist and hauled her upright, catching her round the waist as she scrambled up.

'I'm sorry. I didn't mean to startle you.'

She managed a shaky laugh. 'It d-doesn't matter.'

Even in her half-drowned state, she was pretty, with a heart-shaped face and cornflower eyes. Her teeth were chattering, in spite of the sun, and it struck him that she was not as young as he had originally thought, not a girl at all, but a lady of marriageable age.

'We'd better get back to dry land,' he said.

Hampered by his waterlogged boots, he led the way, glancing back at every step to make sure she was following. She was impeded by her draperies, which swirled around her in the current. Andrew clambered out, then turned to pull her on to the bank.

'Th-thank you,' she said.

'Not at all. It's my fault you fell.'

She murmured a denial and reluctantly he released her. She took a step back from him and leaned forward to inspect the damage. Her dove-grey gown and matching petticoat were drenched and she had fallen on her hat, breaking the brim in two places.

'All this trouble for nothing,' she said ruefully, poking the battered hat.

'You must allow me to buy you a new one.'

'Indeed, sir, that's not necessary.'

'I insist.'

'Hadn't you better empty out your boots?' She changed the subject hastily.

Andrew struggled out of his coat and wrapped it round her shoulders, despite her protests. She hunkered down on the tree stump, leaving enough room for him to perch beside her. There was an abashed silence while he pulled off his sodden stockings. The breeze blew through his shirtsleeves, another forbidden intimacy in polite society, and he couldn't help comparing his ugly feet with her dainty toes. Perhaps she noticed his gaze because she drew her feet beneath the wet, heavy folds of her petticoats.

'We are a pretty pair, aren't we?' he said, tilting back his left boot and watching the water drip into the grass.

She laughed and seemed about to reply when suddenly she whipped her head over her shoulder to stare into the trees.

'What is it?' he asked, instantly alert.

'I thought I heard someone,' she said, standing up and clutching his coat tighter at the neck. Andrew rose too and scanned the shaded area.

'I don't see anyone,' he said.

But his companion had sat down again and begun discreetly drying her feet with her handkerchief.

'I ought to go,' she said. 'I've been away too long already.'

'Must you?' He felt suddenly bereft. He checked himself with an effort. 'Do you have far to go?'

'No, not very,' she replied, glancing at her stockings. Andrew guessed she was too shy to don them while he was watching and he found himself tempted to keep them hostage so he might talk to her a little longer.

'What on earth were you doing here, all on your own?'

'My mistress said she wouldn't need me for a few hours because she was consulting her lawyer,' she said. 'I needed some air and came further than I intended and when the breeze tore my hat off, I had to try to rescue it.' She bit her lip. 'A most unladylike way to behave, I know, but I thought no-one would see me and — '

'I admire your enterprising spirit, Miss — ?'

'Hancock.' She turned a deeper shade of red and lifted her hand to her hair, which had come loose from its knot in curling wisps. 'Leah Hancock.'

Andrew bowed as gallantly as he could, given that he was still barefoot and in his shirtsleeves. 'Andrew Melbury at your service, madam.'

'Melbury?' she repeated. 'Oh.'

And her face closed up. Andrew felt as if a cloud had blotted out the sun.

'You are perhaps familiar with Mrs Melbury, who lives nearby?' he suggested.

She gave him another rueful smile.

'Oh, yes, I am acquainted with her.'

'My grandmother,' he explained. 'I shall be staying with her for a few weeks, perhaps a month. I hope we will meet again in that time?'

'It's not impossible,' she agreed, gazing sidelong at her shoes.

He knew he ought to withdraw discreetly, but instead he blurted out, 'Perhaps you would permit me to accompany you part of the way home?'

She shook her head. 'Better not. I cannot afford to lose my reputation and I'm in a bad enough plight as it is if anyone should catch me. I trust I shall be fairly dry by the time I get back and perhaps I can steal in through the kitchen and escape detection that way.'

She gave him a comical smile and Andrew thought that that was when he lost his heart to her completely.

She returned his coat and he murmured something about seeing to his horse. He couldn't help reproaching himself for not slaking its thirst sooner. His feet felt oddly tender as he made his way across the grass. He took his time, though the urge to glance back was intolerable. Now she must be pulling on her stockings, now tying her garters, now fastening her shoes. The image of her feet in the rippling stream teased him.

But when he finally turned, hoping for a few more words, if only to discover who her employer was, she had vanished as if she had never been there.

★   ★   ★

The rest of Andrew's journey was extremely uncomfortable. He loitered till his horse had drunk its fill, but then could not bear inactivity any longer. While his stockings were nearly dry from the sun, his boots were not and soon enough his feet were soaked again.

He urged his steed on, vainly hoping to catch another glimpse of Leah Hancock. A redbrick house emerged briefly between banks of trees, before it disappeared from sight until he rounded the final bend of the drive.

He had obviously dawdled longer than he thought. His valet had arrived with his trunk and the house was in turmoil at his delay. The butler made no comment about his mistress's state of mind, but the speed with which Andrew was ushered into the drawing room was suggestive.

'Grandmamma, how well you look.'

Mrs Melbury was, as always, dressed in mourning, though it was many years since Andrew's grandfather had died.

'Small thanks to you,' she retorted, haughtily offering him two gnarled and heavily-ringed fingers to kiss. 'I was convinced you had been thrown from your horse or attacked by footpads and left for dead in a ditch. You were just as bad as a boy. I had expected you would grow out of it.'

Andrew let her scold. In spite of everything, he had always been some-thing of a favourite with her and he knew that, underneath her fierce façade, she was flattered by his greeting. The conversation turned to more general topics, particularly the temerity of the Americans in declaring their independence.

'You mark my words, they'll come to rue that piece of folly soon enough,' Mrs Melbury said, wagging her head.

He was spared the need to reply by the arrival of the tea tray. The butler cleared his throat.

'I thought, madam, you'd like to know that Miss Hancock has returned and wishes to know whether her services are required.'

Andrew started at the sound of that name. Everything became clear, especially the stranger's reaction to his name. He was used to a long succession of dark-clad, silent figures gliding in and out of his grandmother's rooms, fetching fans and medicines, adjusting fire screens, opening and closing windows, writing letters from dictation and reading aloud. But on his visits to Herefordshire, he never seemed to meet the same lady's companion twice and had long ceased to notice names or faces.

It seemed a painfully long time before his grandmother spoke, but he could feel her bristling with indignation.

'You'd better send her in,' she replied in repressive tones.

Leah Hancock's gaze was lowered when she entered, but Andrew saw her blush as she caught sight of him. He didn't usually pay much attention to clothes, but he noticed that she had changed into a deep blue gown that brought out golden lights in her hair and emphasised the startling colour of her eyes, when she ventured to raise them.

'Well, Miss Hancock, so you deigned to return,' Mrs Melbury began. 'I suppose we should be grateful for that. What excuse do you have for your delinquency?'

The lady's companion curtsied. 'I'm very sorry, madam. I have no excuse, save that I lost track of time. If you will forgive me, I promise it will never happen again.'

'Humph. If it does, you know what to expect. I don't pay you to go traipsing about the countryside like a hoyden. I had thought a parson's daughter would know how to behave. Obviously I was mistaken.'

Leah Hancock listened to her tirade in silence. Andrew longed to intercede, but he knew his efforts would be useless. Whatever happened, nobody must discover that they had already met under such unusual circumstances.

'Well, don't stay there like a post,' Mrs Melbury snapped. 'Pour the tea — it's getting cold.'

Andrew's eyes met Leah Hancock's for a moment as she brought him his cup. He tried to look sympathetic and the ghost of a mischievous smile flickered across her face so quickly that afterwards he wondered if he had imagined it.

★ ★ ★

Without warning, Andrew was jerked out of his reverie. The coach juddered to a halt as a man's voice called out. Before he had time to gather his wits sufficiently to realise what was happening, the door closest to Leah was wrenched open.

Andrew started forward instinctively, wanting to shield her with his body, but the sight of a pistol pointed directly at Leah stopped him.

'Don't move!'

'Don't hurt my wife!'

Both men cried out simultaneously. Andrew sank back into his seat. He could not risk Leah's life. He squeezed her hand to reassure her. She looked ashen in the moonlight, but externally she remained calm. Only a faint tremor betrayed her.

A half-mask concealed the top part of the highwayman's face. He kept the long barrel of his pistol trained on the same target, knowing that Andrew would not dare reach for his loaded travelling pistols while his wife's life was threatened.

'You know what I want,' the highway-man said, holding out his free hand.

Andrew let go of Leah's hand to fumble for his pocketbook and watch, but the robber rejected the latter, knowing it could be too easily identi-fied. Instead he motioned with his pistol.

'Earrings.'

Leah obeyed, but a hiss of pain told Andrew her hands were shaking so much that she had ripped her earlobe. The earrings too had been a wedding gift and he felt rage begin to well up inside him. What right had anyone to do this?

Leah leaned forward to drop her purse and the gold hoops on to the highwayman's outstretched palm. His horse tossed its head. The moon sprang out from behind a cloud, bathing them in eerie, blue-white light, and she caught a closer look at his face.

'Damn you, don't look at me!'

But Leah stared as if frozen. Andrew's heart contracted into a fist.

'Leah, come away,' he murmured, sliding his arm around her waist to draw her back and at the same moment, she uttered a single word.

'Jack.'

The robber's face seemed to undergo a change at this syllable. The hand that held the pistol twitched. Andrew saw it happening slowly, so slowly, but he was powerless to prevent it. There was a puff of smoke. A tongue of flame dazzled him. Then the noise ripped through the confined space of the coach, echoing round and round his head.

'Leah!' he shouted.

But she had already hunched under the impact with a cry.

2

He heard the noise and confusion from a great distance. Someone uttered a low curse, hooves drummed, then another shot was fired and another. Men shouted. The lady's maid screamed.

But Andrew had no time to reach for his pistols. All his thoughts were absorbed by the beloved but motionless figure in his arms. Please God, let her not be dead. You could not be so cruel as to take her away from me.

'Leah, speak to me. Tell me you're still alive.'

She tilted her head so she could look up at his face. Her lips moved and he barely caught his name. Her right hand crept towards her opposite shoulder.

Her heart. The villain had been aiming for her heart.

'A light, a light,' he shouted. 'My wife's been shot.'

The carriage lamp, wrenched down from its bracket by the valet, dazzled Andrew.

'I think I hit him, sir,' the man gabbled. 'He was fleeing and I can't be sure because of the shadows, but I think I hit him.'

The valet stopped. His eyes, like those of his master, froze on the dark stain on Leah's riding jacket, made visible by the lamplight. Andrew fumbled for his handkerchief to staunch the bleeding. Leah flinched beneath the pressure of his hand and he guessed he had found the wound.

'Send the postilion on ahead to raise the alarm and fetch a surgeon,' Andrew ordered, 'then tell the coachman to get us to the nearest town. She's bleeding to death.'

The door slammed and the valet stumbled away with the lamp, plunging the interior of the coach into darkness. One of the horses was unhitched and Andrew heard its hooves drumming away along the turnpike road. At last the coach lurched forward. Leah gasped and Andrew felt a fresh surge of blood between his fingers.

'There, there, it'll soon be over. We'll get you to safety and a surgeon will see to you and . . . ' The words did not seem to want to cross his stiff lips.

Leah did not reply, but she covered the hand that held the handkerchief with her own. While she continued stroking his knuckles, Andrew knew she was still conscious and alive.

He did not know when the rage began to bubble up again, the sheer, blind hatred of the man who had done this to Leah. But he knew this anger had to be kept in check until the nightmare journey was over. He strove to murmur only reassurances and words of love, but other thoughts kept intruding.

'Not much farther, darling.' How much farther could this confounded forest stretch? He was a stranger to these parts, though Leah had grown up nearby.

He leaned forward and kissed her fervently, cradling her closer. Once he had started kissing her, he could not stop. Every part of her was precious because he might lose her.

Leah's head seemed heavy on his shoulder. Could she be slipping away into sleep and death?

'Don't die, Leah. Please don't die.'

She roused herself with an effort, raising her sagging head.

'I'll do my best,' she said and he was almost certain she made a pained attempt at her usual comical smile.

He scarcely noticed that the wheels and hooves had begun to make a different noise. Lights flashed past the windows and made him blink. Stunned, Andrew raised his head and realised they had finally reached a town. A moment later the coach turned into the yawning arch that led to the yard of the substantial inn.

Dazed by the lights and the noise, Andrew scrambled out. Rejecting all offers of assistance, he lifted Leah out himself and carried her into the inn. The postilion must have done his job because when he asked for a room, the landlord interrupted.

'Yes, yes, sir. Come this way. It's all prepared. The surgeon will be here by and by.'

Andrew followed him through the fumes of the taproom, where the collected populace had become suddenly alert and interested in the novel spectacle and the gabbled tale he found himself repeating. Only when he laid Leah gently on the bed did it occur to him that they had no money with which to pay for this room and the surgeon and everything else, unless he pawned his watch.

It was a shock to see by candlelight the blood-soaked handkerchief clutched in his fingers. But the most horrifying sight was Leah's riding jacket, stiff with blood. She had closed her eyes against the intrusive light and her lips looked pale. Could she be dead?

Terrified, he brushed away the

servants and landlord and ripped open the brass buttons of her jacket and waistcoat. He fumbled with the laces of her stays and discovered her shift had stuck to her skin.

Hands took hold of him from behind, drawing him away.

'You'd best let me see to this,' a man said.

Dully Andrew realised that this must be the surgeon. His head twisted over his shoulder as he was bundled away, his eyes straining towards Leah, terrified that the next time he saw her, she would be dead. As if sensing his gaze, she raised heavy eyelids and stretched out her right arm.

'Don't leave me, Andrew.'

He was at her bedside like a shot, this time on the opposite side to the doctor. 'I won't. I promise. I'll never leave you, never.'

The fingers that curled around his seemed waxen and fragile. Dread lay in his breast like a stone. She had turned her head away from the doctor, as if all hope lay in keeping her eyes on her husband's face. As if in this way she could cheat pain and death.

Andrew held her gaze and forced himself to smile. But out of the corner of his eye, he was aware of the doctor cleaning and probing the wound with his blunt fingers and sharp instruments, striving to extract the slippery bullet.

Sweat broke out on Leah's brow and every now and then she uttered a moan.

I know so little about her. I don't know what she is capable of. And the nagging whisper that had tormented him ever since she uttered that name in the coach crept into his mind.

Who is Jack? He had no doubt the name was the correct one. If she had not recognised the highwayman, if he had not known her, this would not have happened.

Andrew's fingers tightened round hers. Perhaps Leah was not safe even now. The villain had tried to kill her once, afraid she would identify him and send him to the gallows. What was to stop him from trying again, when he realised Leah was still alive and a threat to him?

'There we are.'

Something clattered into a dish.

'If you'll support her, sir, I'll put on a dressing and then she'll be able to rest.'

Leah shuddered, but she allowed herself to be hauled upright. She leaned against her husband while the doctor clamped a pad of lint to the wound and began to wind a bandage under her arm and over her shoulder to secure it.

That done, Andrew lowered Leah on to her pillows and followed the surgeon to a nearby table, where he was wiping and putting away his instruments.

'How bad is it?' he asked in a low tone.

The surgeon paused in his task and glanced at his patient. 'Grave enough,' he said. 'The wound is deep, but at least the ball missed her heart and lungs. Broken bones will mend, if infection doesn't set in, though it's possible that arm and shoulder may remain stiff for the remainder of her natural life.'

Andrew felt ice congeal around his heart.

'How long have you been married to Miss Hancock?'

He was too numb to be surprised by the question. 'Not long,' he replied. Then gathering his wits, he added, 'I'd appreciate it if you said nothing about the identity of your patient until I've informed her family.'

'Of course.'

Everything else Andrew intended to say was driven out of his head by a sharp sob behind him. For the first time since her ordeal began, Leah had given way. He flew back to her side, murmuring reassurances. Large tears oozed between her quivering lashes. Andrew gripped her hand and wiped her tears, but he had never felt so helpless in his life.

★ ★ ★

Leah cried wordlessly but relentlessly for an hour after her maid had helped her into her nightgown and brushed out her golden-brown hair. In the end, Andrew could not bear her grief any longer and gave her a few drops of laudanum to help her sleep, as the doctor had advised before leaving. But now Leah's death-like stillness tormented him.

He was dragged unwillingly away from her by the news that the local magistrate, Mr Barrowcliff, wished to speak to him.

'I'm sorry to disturb you like this,' the bluff, elderly squire said, 'and I'm sorry this should've happened in the first place. But if we're to catch the villain, we have to know as much as possible.'

'Of course,' Andrew murmured mechanically.

'I've already spoken to the servants,' Mr Barrowcliff went on, 'but they seem hardly to have seen the man. Can you give any sort of description?'

Moonlight. The shadows of Sherwood Forest. Leah's hand trembling in his, her gasp as she tore her earlobe. And then that noise.

'Mr Melbury?' the magistrate prompted him.

'It was dark. He wore a mask,' Andrew replied dully. 'But my wife recognised him. She called him by name. That's why he shot her.'

'Indeed? And the name?'

'Jack.'

'That's all?'

'That's all.'

Andrew had tried asking Leah about the highwayman, but she had merely shaken her head and grown more distressed.

'I don't suppose I could talk to — '

'No!' Leah had endured enough for one night. 'She's asleep. Maybe tomorrow . . .'

The magistrate submitted. 'Well, if you could coax the surname out of her, I'll write out the warrant for his arrest in the wink of an eye.' Mr Barrowcliff promised, clasping his hand warmly.

'Her father might know, or her sister,' Andrew said and then shivered at the thought that he would have to tell his unknown-in-laws what had happened. 'Her maiden name was Hancock.'

'Not the parson's daughter?'

'Yes.'

The magistrate puckered her lips as if about to whistle in surprise and then thought better of it. 'I never knew she were wed.'

'Only three days ago.'

Andrew was aware that the older man muttered something sympathetic, but his thoughts had already drifted. Mr Barrowcliff's next words caught his attention, however.

'Best not disturb her family tonight,' he suggested. 'It's late and unless there's any immediate danger, tomorrow morn's soon enough for bad news.'

Andrew seized on the excuse gratefully. He could not cope with any more strangers just now.

'At dawn, I'll take my servants and

the constable and anyone else that'll come and see if we can't find any tracks in the wood. I've sent urgent messages to all the turnpikes and larger towns and villages in the county to keep their eyes open for any suspicious characters. I doubt he'll escape hanging when we do catch him.'

A fierce surge deep inside him frightened Andrew. He had never felt so passionately about anything. Even hanging was too good for the man. He wished he could tear him limb from limb, to make him feel one fraction of the pain he had inflicted.

'It's unusual for a highwayman to strike at full moon.' Mr Barrowcliff shook his head thoughtfully. 'He must be a desperate character to take such a risk. If it had been yesterday, when the Nottingham Assembly was taking place, I could've understood.' But at a glance at Andrew's face, he changed tack. 'I'd best be going. You'll be wanting to return to your wife.'

Long into the dark hours of the night

Andrew sat sleeplessly by the sickbed. He did not want to disturb Leah or move from her side, but at the same time it was hard to sit still, knowing that there was nothing he could do to help or avenge her.

Leah stirred and moaned in her sleep. Andrew leaned forward to stroke her cheek and gently pinch her earlobe. He could feel the hole where the earring ought to have been.

3

Those weeks in Herefordshire seemed both dream-like and vivid to Andrew, remote and yet so recent. It had been strange to find himself living in the same house as Leah Hancock and yet seeing so little of her. In his grandmother's presence, she was little more than a shadow, though now and then he detected a spark of humour in her replies that proved she was not as meek as she pretended to be.

Every family in the neighbourhood rallied to pay calls on Mrs Melbury and her grandson and invited them to dinners and excursions. Mrs Melbury was not always well enough to go and she insisted that Andrew should deliver her apologies in person. But all the while he was out, supposedly enjoying himself, he found his mind straying back to Leah, to whom such amusements were denied.

Even when he stayed with his grandmother, there were other torments to endure. She did not spare Leah any more than she had spared her previous companions. Andrew knew it would be worse than useless to intervene directly. Mrs Melbury had sharp ears, sharp eyes and an even sharper tongue if she thought she detected the least impropriety between her grandson and a young person she considered his inferior.

But over the years he had devised a number of stratagems with which to distract his grandmother. At times she forgot to tyrannise her underling while she regaled her grandson with malicious gossip about her dearest friends and nearest neighbours, or reminisced about the illustrious conquests of her youth.

At such moments she seemed not to notice that Andrew was stealing glances at Leah, who was diligently sewing shirts for the poor of the parish for which Mrs Melbury would take sole credit since she had chosen and paid for the material.

Occasionally, while Andrew was reading aloud, Mrs Melbury would doze off, or at least appear to do so. It wasn't safe to make too many assumptions. Andrew once broke off reading in such circumstances to ask Leah a question. Before she could answer, a spectral voice interrupted.

'I can still hear you, young man. And I'll thank you to keep your mind on your own task, instead of distracting Miss Hancock from hers.'

'I'm sorry, Grandmamma. I promise not to do it again,' Andrew replied, trying to ignore the mischievous smile tugging at Leah's lips.

However, if Mrs Melbury's mouth fell open and she began snoring, he was pretty certain she really was asleep, because nothing would have induced her to do something so undignified voluntarily. Then he ventured to talk to Leah, always keeping a wary eye on his grandmother and his finger at roughly

36

the point in the text where he had left off.

Andrew took to strolling or riding out whenever his grandmother was resting and might have sent her companion out on an errand. The first time he encountered Leah this way, he was startled to find her wearing a plain, battered hat. He had not intended to say anything, but she noticed his askance look.

'I borrowed it from the cook,' she explained, touching the brim self-consciously, but smiling her comical smile. 'I was to have gone into Hereford with the butcher's cart yesterday to buy a new hat, but Mrs Melbury found she could not spare me after all.'

Andrew assumed that Leah would be granted another half-holiday, but nothing happened. Eventually, finding himself alone with Mrs Melbury, he could not resist inquiring casually what day Miss Hancock would be free so he could spend the afternoon entertaining his grandmother.

'Oh, not till next week,' Mrs Melbury

replied. 'If she chooses to go gallivanting when she is meant to be at work, she must face the consequences.'

The result was that on Sunday, the cook needed her own hat and Leah was obliged to go to church in the ugliest of her mistress's cast-offs and endure the older neighbours' praises for Mrs Melbury's generosity and the sneers of more fashionable ladies.

That was the final straw. Early next morning, Andrew set out for Hereford in Mrs Melbury's chaise.

Even at the time it struck him as ludicrous that he promenaded past the milliner's shop three times before he summoned enough courage to enter. As luck would have it, the shop was empty, save for a shop-girl, who was tidying away wares rejected by a previous customer.

Once he had fixed on his choice — a small chip hat covered with white silk and trimmed with blue ribbon and white feathers — there was still the painfully slow rigmarole of wrapping the hat in a paper-lined box, which was then tied with stout ribbon, before the shop-girl counted out his change with painstaking exactness.

When he finally found himself out on the street, his predicament was even worse. The burden he was carrying was so obviously a hatbox, he felt very conspicuous as he threw himself into the chaise and ordered it home. Nor was it easy to smuggle the hat into the house and find a moment to intercept Leah.

'Oh, sir,' she stammered. 'It's very generous, but you shouldn't have gone to this expense. Think of the impropriety.'

'Impropriety be hanged. No-one need know I gave it to you. And after all I have suffered, I should think it's the least you can do to accept my sacrifice with good grace.'

He told her the whole tragicomic tale and she laughed and murmured sympathetic words that were balm to his soul.

'When you put your case so forcefully, I don't see how I can refuse,' she said, a troubled look still shading her eyes. 'Only it's much too grand for me.'

Disappointment gushed into his throat. He could see she was right. The hat seemed over-elaborate now he compared its feathers and frills with her plain gown. All he had thought of when he chose it was how well the blue ribbon would match her eyes.

'Oh, sir, don't look so downcast. It really is beautiful, only I don't think Mrs Melbury would approve. Unless perhaps I could remove the feathers?' She glanced up, seeking his permission.

'By all means.'

'I suppose we could pretend that my sister sent it to me and you fetched it from the post office. But you must allow me to pay for it.'

He demurred, she insisted, and in the end they compromised. He reluctantly accepted half the cost of the hat out of her meagre wages on the grounds that she would have had to buy one herself, though she might not have chosen such an expensive one.

It seemed to Andrew that from that moment there was a new intimacy between them, more conspiratorial smiles and coded messages exchanged within casual conversation.

★　★　★

His whole body convulsed. For a few seconds Andrew was disorientated. Then he realised he had fallen asleep in his chair.

The anxiety that had kept him awake for the best part of the night propelled him to Leah's bedside, though his head spun and his eyes were sore from lack of sleep.

He could not help himself. He touched her cheek. It was warm and she rolled her head towards him. Heavy lashes fluttered and his conscience smote him.

'Andrew?' Her voice was muffled.

'Ssh, darling. I'm sorry for waking you. Go back to sleep.'

But her eyes opened wider in

between slow blinks, as if she wanted to focus her gaze on his face.

'Such a bad dream,' she murmured.

'Never mind. It's gone now. I'm here to protect you.'

She smiled heavily. Better that she thought it was a dream for now. Better that she should rest. There would be time enough for her to remember.

'Kiss me, Andrew.'

He obeyed, then closed her eyes with two more kisses.

'Go back to sleep.'

Who is Jack? He bit back the question. Every moment the highwayman might be getting further away, out of the reach of justice. Mr Barrowcliff and his underlings would already be out in the forest. If he could have been sure there was no danger this Jack would double back and find a way to kill Leah, Andrew would have gone with them. But he knew he would not have a moment's peace if he left Leah with only servants and strangers to protect her.

As he watched her lapsing into sleep, it occurred to him that although he was a stranger in Framworth, Leah was not. He ought to warn her family before rumour caught up with them.

It was not an easy letter to write, especially as he felt so sluggish. When he reread it afterwards, he was not even capable of deciding whether it was coherent. But he was too distracted to make another attempt and so he signed and sealed it before dispatching Betty, Leah's maid, to find someone to deliver it to the parsonage.

The address reminded him of the letter he had written four days ago, informing Mr Hancock that he and Leah had been married at Hereford by special licence and intended to come to Framworth. How much had changed since then.

Inactivity and the absence of news maddened him. Inevitably his thoughts turned backwards.

★ ★ ★

It was hard to imagine it was only a week since the meeting in the copse. He had been sauntering about the garden before dinner when he caught sight of a slender figure. Even from a distance, he could not be mistaken about its identity, even if he had not seen the blue hat ribbons flaring out behind her.

She vanished among the trees. Andrew barely hesitated before he followed. He guessed she was going to the rustic bench a little farther on. He was tempted to creep up behind her like a child, cover her eyes with his hands and make her guess who it was. Already he could imagine the softness of her skin, the flutter of her lashes on his palms, perhaps her fingers wrestling his away. She would blush and laugh and perhaps, perhaps he would tell her how much he loved her . . .

The trees rustled, masking his footfalls. A noise made him stop and listen. At first he thought he had imagined it. Then it was repeated. Leah's voice, a tiny, bubbling sound. Stifled giggles.

Did she know he was there?

He edged closer to the bench and, as he had expected, caught a glimpse of her beribboned hat, the tip of her shoe, the hem of her gown. And then he froze. The noise was now more distinct, unmistakable. Leah was not laughing, but crying, strangled sobs that wrung his heart.

He did not allow himself to think. In an instant he was seated beside her, holding her hands and begging her not to be alarmed, but to tell him what was wrong.

'If there is anything in my power . . . '

He could see from her expression she was overwhelmed by the suddenness of his appearance, but she made no attempt to remove her hands from his grasp. Tears glistened on her cheeks and her lips trembled as she groped for words.

'You — you are very kind,' she stammered, 'but I cannot . . . '

'Is it my grandmother? Has she been unkind to you?'

'No, no, it's nothing.' She withdrew one hand to brush away her tears.

Andrew took a deep breath. He must remember he was a gentleman. He must on no account take advantage of her vulnerability. If he rashly declared his feelings and she did not return them, it would put her in a very awkward position. And yet he could not seem to let go of her hand.

'I ought to go,' she said, but as she rose, something white tumbled from her lap.

Andrew stopped to pick it up. It was a letter, scrawled in handwriting so jagged, he was surprised anyone had been able to decipher the address.

'I'm sorry. I didn't mean to pry,' he murmured as he passed the letter back to Leah, aware he had stared at it too long.

She managed a tremulous smile. 'It doesn't matter.'

But clearly it did. Her eyes were welling up again.

'Bad news?' he ventured.

'My father and I — have been estranged for some years. When I recognised his handwriting, I hoped he might have forgiven me, but . . . ' She bit her lip. 'I've been corresponding secretly with my sister, but he found out and has forbidden it.'

No wonder she was upset. He could not imagine what terrible misdemeanour she could have committed to merit being disowned.

'He disapproves of my present occupation,' Leah said, obviously feeling she owed him an explanation. 'He wanted me to — to make a socially advantageous match instead.'

'I see.'

But he knew there must be something more and he suspected that she knew he was trying hard not to speculate.

'Sometimes I think it would have been easier to give way and do what everybody wanted me to do,' she said with sudden vehemence. 'At least then — '

47

'You did the right thing,' he said gently. 'You would have despised yourself if you had made a mercenary match.'

'Yes,' she replied, but she sounded vague.

'Marriage without love, or at very least esteem, must be terrible, don't you think?' he urged, hoping to discover her principles matched his own.

'Ah, love,' she sighed. 'I wish — I wish I could trust the dictates of my heart. But experience has taught me I am a poor judge of character when I am blinded by emotion.'

There was some mystery here, some unhappy or unrequited love of her youth.

'I find it difficult to believe. You have always struck me as being very measured in your judgements.'

'I see I have deceived you too,' Leah replied, attempting a laugh. Then she seemed to shake herself. 'I really must return to the house.'

'So must I. I hope you won't object

to my accompanying you?'

In hindsight, Andrew realised they had been watched as they crossed the lawn together. Perhaps his grandmother herself had seen them. She was more snappish and unreasonable than usual that evening and he was hard pressed to keep her distracted from Leah, who was closer to tears than Mrs Melbury's lectures had ever made her before. But it was not till the following afternoon that the executioner's axe fell.

4

It had been a disappointing ride. Andrew had failed to meet Leah along the way, but he consoled himself that he would see her at dinner. He was brought up short outside the house. Mrs Melbury's chaise was waiting there while two servants hauled a modest trunk on to its roof. Seized by a sudden foreboding, Andrew leapt from his saddle.

At exactly the same moment, the front door opened and Leah staggered out, her eyes glazed. She was wearing her riding habit. At the sight of Andrew, she flushed and he had the impression that she would have liked to move towards the chaise without uttering a word.

'Miss Hancock, whatever is the matter?'

She glanced over her shoulder and,

following her gaze, Andrew realised his grandmother was standing at the window of the study. Then Leah uttered the words he dreaded the most.

'I've been dismissed,' she said, through stiff, pale lips.

'Dismissed?' A cold wave lapped over him. He had always known it was a possibility, given his grandmother's temperament, but the suddenness shook him. There ought to have been some warning. 'What on earth for?'

She would not meet his eye and it only confirmed his conviction that he had been indiscreet and her reputation had suffered.

'It's my fault, isn't it?'

'No.' Leah bit her lip and looked away. 'She accused me of stealing.'

'Stealing? Stealing what?'

'I'm accused of stealing her most prized possession — her grandson.'

Andrew was left open-mouthed.

'Of course it is a ridiculous allegation,' Leah went on in a bright, tight tone. 'I know better than to look so far

above me, especially as she thinks . . . '
She broke off abruptly and changed
tack. 'But one excuse will serve as well
as another if she is determined to get
rid of me.'

'It's not ridiculous. I am in love with
you . . . ' Andrew stopped himself. This
was not how he had intended to declare
his feelings, with two servants within
earshot and his grandmother glaring at
them from a window.

Even as the thought crossed his
mind, an imperious voice called from
the door.

'Andrew!'

'Let me talk to you in private,' he
said, ignoring his grandmother's sum-
mons. Leah's head was bowed. The
very hat he had bought for her hid her
face. Despair filled his heart. She does
not care for me as I care for her.

'I cannot.'

'Please, Leah, listen to — '

'Andrew, come away at once! I must
speak to you.'

Torn, Andrew glanced back. Mrs

Melbury stood at the top of the steps, a small but formidable figure framed by the portico.

'At least wait for me,' he begged. 'I'll talk to her. I'll explain everything.'

Explain what, you presumptuous fool? You have embarrassed the woman you love. She does not return your feelings. You are putting her in an impossible situation . . .

His name was called again.

'Go, go,' Leah urged. 'You mustn't anger her, not for my sake. I'll wait.' She gave him such an imploring look that he obeyed.

There was no mistaking his grandmother's anger.

'How could you make such a spectacle of yourself in front of the servants?' she demanded as the study door shut behind them. 'And over such a worthless baggage.'

'You've no right to blacken Miss Hancock's name,' he retorted, too loudly to be discreet. 'I defy you to find one instance in which she has behaved contrary to the dictates of morality.'

Mrs Melbury smiled triumphantly and suddenly Andrew felt sick with dread. Did she know something he did not?

'Oh, indeed, sir? What would you say about a young woman who makes clandestine assignations to meet men without a chaperone? Who was seen by reliable witnesses in a half-naked state in public?'

Andrew reeled. His grandmother took advantage of his silence to go on.

'Your virtuous Miss Hancock has been seen by the river, barefoot as a gypsy, in the company of a man, and I am informed that that ridiculously extravagant hat she flaunts in the face of the world was a gift from one of her paramours.'

'I don't know who your informant is,' Andrew said, trying to keep his tone steady, 'but I don't suppose they told you who the man in question was.'

'The man is irrelevant. A young woman lacking in virtue has no place in my home.'

'Both these incidents have an innocent explanation. I know that because I was there. I came across Miss Hancock by chance when she was trying to rescue her hat from the river. I bought a new hat on her behalf, solely because you would not allow her a half-holiday to purchase one herself. And since her reputation is apparently so blighted, I intend to make amends by marrying her, if she will have me.'

At his last words, the old woman turned on him and he was stunned to see how pale and tremulous she had grown.

'You cannot mean that. You're only saying it to spite me.'

'Oh no, I mean every word of it. I had not intended to speak to Miss Hancock yet. I had hoped to engage her heart before then, but this has only hastened my resolve.'

He turned towards the door.

'Andrew, don't be a fool,' she shrieked. 'Can't you see the fortune hunter planned it from the start? She set out to bewitch you and throw you into compromising situations.'

He did not stop to listen, but her words echoed across the wide marble vestibule.

'If you do this, you will live to regret it. You mark my words.' And then a plaintive cry. 'Andrew, my boy, don't leave me.'

But her voice was drowned out by a louder, closer noise. The crunch of wheels through gravel, the thud of hooves. He had delayed too long.

The carriage had not yet picked up speed and still had the curve of the drive to negotiate. He took the shortest route across the grass, running as fast as he could, calling to the coachman to stop. He had almost reached them; his hands were stretching out to grapple with the carriage door. He could not breathe; he could not keep this up. He would be forced to drop back. With his last breath, he cried out one last time.

The chaise lurched to a halt. Panting and incredulous, Andrew stumbled forward to lean against the carriage. Leah's pale face was gazing out at him. Somehow he yanked open the door and clambered in without lowering the steps. Leah drew herself to the furthest corner. Her hand stretched out for the opposite door as if preparing to flee.

'I'm sorry. I didn't mean to frighten you,' he gasped. 'Please, hear me out.'

'Don't try to speak yet.' She released the door and reached out as if to touch his arm, but stopped short at the last moment.

'You promised to wait.'

'I know. I'm sorry. I lost my nerve. I thought it would be easier this way.'

It was dark inside the chaise and he realised why it had stopped here. The trees that grew along the drive screened the carriage from prying eyes. After his previous blunder, Andrew hardly knew how to begin.

'Where are you going?'

'Hereford.'

'You have friends there?'

She shook her head. 'I intend to take

the first outside place I can get on any coach going north or east. If I can reach Birmingham, it should not be difficult to get another coach to Nottingham or perhaps Leicester or Derby.'

'You're going back to Nottinghamshire?'

'There's nothing else I can do.'

'And what if your father does not forgive you?'

She winced. He had not intended to hurt her, but he was worried about her.

'I don't know,' she said at last, staring at her hands. 'It's possible some old friends might help. I haven't had time to think yet.'

He knew without being told that she could not have much money. The journey would be expensive, slow and quite possibly hazardous, especially to a lady travelling on her own. And without a letter of recommendation, how would she find work? Would even old friends look at her askance?

'No, I cannot let you do this,' he said. 'It's my fault your reputation has been

58

tarnished. Let me make amends. Marry me.'

He found he was clasping her hands, though he could not remember when he had taken hold of them. She looked up at him with an uncertain laugh.

'You shouldn't joke about such things. I might take you seriously.'

'Good. I mean every word.'

'But we hardly know each other.'

'I know enough. I know you are courageous and witty and unfailingly patient with cantankerous old ladies. I swear to you, I have no major vices — I only drink moderately and hardly ever play cards and never for high stakes.'

Incredulous eyes scanned his face. 'This is madness.'

'Not at all. We are both of age and I have a comfortable income from my property in Leicestershire. I suspect there is no hope of a legacy from my grandmother, but I can support a wife and family perfectly well without it. All very practical and prudent, but — '

But you don't love me, do you? The

question gnawed at him. He could feel cracks forming in the dam that kept his feelings in check. Little trickles of despair had begun to seep into his heart, heralding an imminent deluge.

'Oh, sir, I don't doubt your generosity,' she said, dropping her gaze. 'God knows I have seen enough examples of it. But I cannot let you sacrifice yourself in this way — '

'It's not a sacrifice and there is nothing unselfish about my offer,' Andrew interrupted impetuously. 'I think about you night and day. I cannot sleep, I cannot eat — I cannot bear to live without you.'

He was seized by a sudden doubt. Had he frightened her with his vehemence?

'This is your cue, Miss Hancock, to tell me how flattered you are, but unfortunately you cannot return my sentiments.'

Her fingers clasped his tighter. Her voice was barely audible. 'No, that's one lie I cannot utter.'

The warmth of hope began to pulse through his veins.

'Then you do love me?' he asked, leaning closer.

'Yes.'

He might not have caught the whisper if he had been further away.

'And you will marry me?'

'Ah, you should not tempt a poor girl beyond her endurance.'

'But you will marry me?'

'It's not that simple. Your grand-mother will despise me as a fortune hunter.'

'What does that matter when we know the truth?'

She gazed at him with haunted eyes and still she would not say the word. Another twinge of doubt seized him.

'You do love me, don't you?' he repeated.

'Yes, oh yes.'

'Then why should we hesitate?'

'I — you must forgive me. I'm not used to — to making such momentous decisions on the spur of the moment. I have always been cautious by nature, perhaps too cautious for my own good, but — ' She was flushed from forehead to neck.

Andrew could not resist temptation. Before she could react, he swooped and kissed her on the lips. 'Now will you marry me?' he asked, his lips brushing hers at every word.

'Yes,' she whispered and he opened her mouth for another kiss.

★   ★   ★

Andrew halted in the midst of his pacing to part the bed curtains. To his surprise, Leah's eyes were open but blank.

'How long have you been awake?' he asked, stroking her hair back from her face.

It took her a moment to reply. 'I don't know. A while.'

'How do you feel? Is the pain very bad?'

'Nothing I can't endure,' she said

with an imitation of her usual smile. 'As long as I don't move.' But she closed her eyes and shivered.

'The doctor says there is a good chance you will make a full recovery. And every effort is being made to capture the man who did this to you,' Andrew said, but her shudders only grew more pronounced.

Alarmed, he placed his hand on her forehead. If she were feverish, it might be a sign that infection was setting in. But her skin felt cool to his touch.

'There's nothing to be frightened of any more,' he went on.

'I know.' She opened her eyes to smile at him again. 'I wish . . . '

'What, darling?'

She hesitated. 'No, nothing.' But she uttered an involuntary groan as she turned her head aside.

'Leah,' he said, lowering his voice, 'I know this is painful to you, but you must tell me the name of the man who shot you.'

A tear trickled between her lashes

and down her cheek. Again she shivered.

'Please, Andrew, don't ask me. It's too awful. I can't.' She gulped and covered her mouth with her hand.

'I'm sorry. I don't want to distress you.' He could not bear to see her cry. 'I only want to help.'

A tap at the door made them both jump. It was only the doctor, come to see how his patient had survived the night. Leah rallied with an effort and answered his questions as succinctly as possible. But Andrew could see that her mind kept drifting.

'Sir?'

The voice startled him. He had not heard the maid enter.

'What is it?' he asked. 'Is there any news?'

'There's — there's a gentleman and a young lady to see you.'

He frowned. Why could not these people let him alone?

'The gentleman, he says his name is Hancock.'

The name echoed twice, thrice through his head before he realised why it was familiar. Leah's father.

No matter how difficult Leah's relationship with her father was, he could not send him away. By the same token, Andrew was reluctant to bring him into the sickroom directly because he could not judge how Mr Hancock would react until he met the man.

'Tell them — no.' He cleared his throat and passed a dry tongue over his lips. 'No, I'd better speak to them myself.'

5

His first impression as he entered the parlour was of an austere, black figure with a hawk-like beak and a domed forehead, which a white bob-wig did nothing to diminish.

'Mr Hancock?' Andrew extended his hand. 'I'm Andrew Melbury.'

The clergyman bowed solemnly, making no attempt to take his hand.

'I wish we could have met in happier circumstances,' he said and Andrew formed the impression those sharp grey eyes took in every detail of his rumpled appearance. 'We came as soon as we received your note.'

Something rustled at the far end of the room. Andrew's eye was drawn to a female figure who had been staring sightlessly out of the window at the activity in the yard.

'My daughter, Jessica.'

Andrew had been expecting a younger version of Leah and there was a resemblance about the mouth and nose. But despite his love for his wife, despite clear signs that Jessica had been crying, he was forced to admit she was by far the prettier sister with her golden curls and huge eyes.

'I'm pleased to meet you at last,' he said. 'Leah has told me a great deal about you.'

Unlike her father, Jessica clasped his proffered hand and then burst into tears.

'She won't die, will she?' she sobbed. 'I couldn't bear it if . . . ' Tears would have stopped her voice, even if her father hadn't intervened.

'Jessica, Jessica, you must not give way like this. Your sister is in God's hands.'

'The doctor assures me there is no sign of infection yet,' Andrew added.

Mr Hancock began pumping him for information about the robbery and what steps had been taken to discover

67

the perpetrator of this monstrous deed. Andrew did his best to oblige, though his instincts urged him to return to his wife as soon as possible. But there was one mystery the Hancocks might be able to solve, thus sparing Leah's feelings.

'She called the highwayman by name — Jack. I though you might know who she meant?'

Father and daughter exchanged blank looks. 'It must be someone she knew well or perhaps a servant since she didn't use a surname,' Andrew suggested.

'Half my parishioners are called John,' Mr Hancock said dubiously. 'There's the butcher's lad and at least a dozen stockingers, and old Jack Dawkins the sexton.'

'Oh, this was a young man, that much I can tell you. All old men and boys with unbroken voices can be safely discounted.'

'Surely the easiest way to resolve this is to ask Leah herself,' Mr Hancock pointed out, barely concealing his impatience.

'Believe me, I have tried, but she is still so distressed by what has happened, I don't want to force her.'

Mr Hancock looked his son-in-law up and down. It was clear he disapproved of Andrew's indulgence of what he considered feminine whims though he did not say so.

'I don't even like leaving her too long,' Andrew went on, hoping they would take the hint.

'Can't we see her?' Jessica burst out. 'Only for a moment?'

'The doctor is with her at present,' Andrew replied, suppressing the urge to refuse. 'But I'll tell her you're here.'

With that he bolted. No wonder Leah had chosen to find paid work rather than live with her father. And no wonder she had often spoken of her fears for her sister.

'I know everyone thinks she is so carefree that nothing can depress her for long,' Leah had said once, 'but Jessica feels Papa's criticisms more deeply than she will admit.'

He half-hoped that the doctor would forbid visitors so he could send the Hancocks away with a clear conscience. But the surgeon merely warned him not to let the patient overexert herself.

There was a rustle of silk as the door opened. Leah stretched out her arm to embrace her sister, though she flinched under the impact.

'I'm so sorry. I didn't mean to hurt you . . . '

'It doesn't matter.' Leah smiled, though she had turned ashen with pain. She gazed at her sister in wonder. 'How tall and beautiful you've grown.'

'What did you expect?' Jessica gurgled, laughter mingling with tears. 'It's been four years.'

In contrast to Jessica's effusiveness, Mr Hancock was aloof and awkward. He made some vague inquiries about Leah's health and stiffly congratulated her on her marriage, while throwing scrutinising looks at Andrew, as if to evaluate whether he was a fit match for his firstborn. But on the whole, he seemed more willing to forgive Leah for her past transgressions, now she was the wife of a wealthy man, than he would have been if she had returned alone, penniless and in disgrace.

Recovering from her false start, Jessica began telling Leah the latest gossip, while their father drew Andrew aside to catechise him about his income, prospects and morals.

While Mr Hancock read the marriage contract that ensured Leah would be well provided for, both as a wife and a widow, Andrew's attention wandered.

'Leah, there's something I must tell you.'

Andrew pricked up his ears. Jessica seemed troubled.

'Mr Ward is at the Grange,' she blurted out, looking down at her hands. 'He's been there nearly two weeks and — and has called at the parsonage a few times and . . . '

'Oh. I hoped — ' All the colour had drained from Leah's face. She tried again. 'I didn't think he came to

71

Framworth much any more.'

'He doesn't. He's been away so long, his aunt threatened to cut him off without a penny. Not, of course, that I believe for a second that that is why he returned.'

'How is he?' Leah's voice was barely audible.

'Much as he always was. He still isn't married, you know.'

Andrew could feel a thousand questions throbbing in his brain. But before he could ask them, he was summoned downstairs to speak to Mr Barrowcliff.

The magistrate had little to report. 'We found this at the scene of the crime,' he said, dropping a single gold earring into Andrew's palm. 'There were signs he made off through the forest, where the bracken was crushed, but it's been so dry of late, there are few hoof prints. I did hear tell of two suspicious-looking characters seen near the forest, but they were apparently on foot and most likely poachers.'

'He could be miles away,' Andrew said in a dull tone. 'We might never catch him.'

'It's beginning to look that way,' Mr Barrowcliff agreed, 'unless Mrs Melbury names the man. Then we could publish a description and offer a reward for information.'

Andrew let the older man accompany him to the sickroom. Leah had asked if the magistrate could be invited upstairs, but he had not dared permit it earlier, afraid the news might be too upsetting for someone in her weakened condition.

Leah sat up as they entered. Even from the doorway, Andrew could see she was trembling. Barely conscious of anyone else, he hurried towards her.

'Lie down, darling. You're cold,' he urged, but Leah resisted.

'Tell me what you know.'

'Nothing. There is no clue, no trail — nothing except one of your earrings. He must have dropped it in his haste to get away.'

She buried her face on his breast and whispered something. It sounded uncannily like, 'Thank God,' but he was sure his ears had deceived him.

Mr Barrowcliff cleared his throat. 'The only way we'll catch the ruffian is if you tell us who he is.'

Andrew felt Leah's body tense in his embrace. Gently he rubbed her back.

'I swear, I won't let him hurt you. We'll catch him and hang him and . . . '

'If you love me, Andrew, please let this go.'

A shadow interposed between them and the light.

'Come, come, child, there is no need for this nonsense,' Mr Hancock said.

'Whatever scruple you have taken into your head, I assured you it is misplaced. Nay, it is your duty to name the villain. Who is he?'

'I don't know.'

The parson's lips compressed. 'I had thought I had brought up my daughters to be truthful. Your husband says you called the highwayman by name. Is he a liar or are you?'

Leah winced. Three voices protested simultaneously, but Mr Hancock ignored them.

'Who is he, Leah?'

'Nobody.'

'Leah.'

'He is nobody. I made a mistake. Why can't you let this rest? Why must you torment me like this?' A broken sob escaped her.

Mr Hancock eyed her coldly. 'I expect such affectations of sensibility from your sister, not from you.'

'Stop it, Papa.' Jessica's voice was shrill with suppressed hysteria.

Andrew could see Mr Hancock was completely oblivious to the effect of his words of his younger daughter. It was high time to intervene.

'I think you ought to leave, sir,' he said, scarcely disguising the coldness in his voice. 'Leah is far too ill to be upset like this.'

Mr Hancock glared at him, drawing himself up to his full height, but Mr

Barrowcliff tugged his sleeve.

'As you wish,' the parson said. 'Come along, Jessica.'

But the door had already slammed behind her. Andrew could hear her stumbling towards the stairs. He wished there was something he could do for her, but he could not leave Leah in her current state. Tear after tear was rolling down her face, all the more eerily because she hardly uttered a sound, apart from the occasional gasp for breath. Mr Barrowcliff mumbled an apology and then he too was gone.

'Leah, darling,' Andrew murmured.

'I don't — I don't want to think about it any more.'

'You don't have to. Not till you're better.'

Her suffering only made him more determined to catch the culprit and make him pay for what he had done. His hands shook as he measured out a dose of laudanum.

'Here, drink this. It will help you sleep.'

Obediently she drained the glass and then looked up at him. 'Will you hold me until I fall asleep?'

He did not need to be asked twice. He manoeuvred himself onto the bed, with his back against the headboard, so she could lay her head on his breast. He encircled her with his arms and tugged the covers up to her chin. On an impulse he bent to kiss her.

'You've no idea how much I want to pick you up and carry you away to the safety of my own home,' he said and began telling her about his house, which she had not yet seen, and all the things she would be mistress of when she was better. Leah listened with a faint smile until her eyes finally dropped shut.

*   *   *

Andrew was not sure afterwards how long he had remained there, gazing at his wife as she slept on his breast. Suddenly, with a grunt of effort, Leah pushed herself upright. Andrew was caught off guard. Only a moment earlier, she had appeared to be in a deep sleep. Now her eyes were wide, but unnaturally bright.

'Where is he?'

'Who?' Andrew asked, though from the sinking sensation in his stomach, he thought he could guess.

'Did he get away? Did you shoot him? Oh, God, oh, God,' she murmured in a rapid underbreath. 'How could this happen?'

She spoke as if she was in a high fever and yet when Andrew touched her, she seemed no warmer than usual.

'Ssh, darling. Calm down. You're safe here. No-one can hurt you.'

She shook her head restlessly. Andrew realised from the look in her eyes that she was still asleep, under the influence of the drug and whatever thoughts had tormented her while she was awake.

'No, it isn't possible,' she murmured as he cradled her against him. 'Shadow . . .'

'Hush, Leah. Don't think about it. Try to forget.'

'Oh God.' She squeezed her eyes shut as if to block out remembrance. 'Jack, Jack, how could you do this to me?'

It was the tone of her voice that sent waves of horror over Andrew. Now at last he understood. Leah wasn't frightened of her attacker. She was grieving because she felt betrayed by someone she trusted. She was protecting her own would-be murderer and that could only mean one thing. She loved this other man.

His thoughts were racing faster and faster until it was impossible to sit still any longer. Leah half-woke as he eased her onto her pillows. He kissed her with numb lips and promised he would not be gone long. Thankfully she was too dulled with sleep to ask questions.

Andrew summoned the maid and valet and left strict instructions that no one was to disturb his wife in his absence. Then he blundered downstairs and out into the bustling marketplace.

He didn't know where he was going, but the sight of a church at the far end of a street drew him on. He sought out the most secluded corner of the graveyard, overlooking the river, and sank down on the wall.

It seemed an oddly appropriate place to come. In a church just four days ago, he had been married and thought himself the luckiest man alive. And now . . . He stared at the gravestones, some new and upright, others grey and sloping at crazy angles. The river whispered sinister secrets.

He remembered the look of doubt in Leah's eyes before she placed her hand in his as they stood before the altar. He remembered the way she hid her blushes on his breast when he first glimpsed her in her nightgown on their wedding night.

Now another possibility tormented him. Had she been reluctant because she was not in love with him?

Leah had risked her father's displeasure to reject a man she did not love. If she had not wanted to marry him, she would not have done so.

Andrew drew in a deep breath. There was no point in sitting here, letting the autumn chill seep into his bones. He had to go back. Just because Leah had decided to shield her assailant did not mean she was safe, he realised. If the villain did not know that nothing would induce her to betray him . . .

The very thought hastened his steps. He only dimly noticed a gentleman who held the door open for him. Andrew thanked him mechanically and began making his way towards the stairs. But an educated voice stopped him in his tracks.

'Do you know — can you tell me, how is the, the lady that was shot?'

6

Andrew turned. The stranger who had arrived at the same time as him was grasping the landlady by the sleeve.

'Is it true?' he continued before the woman could reply. 'Is it really Mr Hancock's daughter?'

'Oh, yes, sir, that's true enough,' she confirmed. 'T' parson's been to see her an' all. She's poorly enough too, so t' doctor says.'

'But not likely to die, surely?'

The stranger's obvious distress kept Andrew rooted to the spot.

'That's more than I can say. You'd have to ask the doctor, or her husband maybe — '

Andrew drew deeper into the shadows, hoping he could not be seen. Questions beat in his forehead. Who was this man? His colourless face was handsome enough, marred only by a weak mouth and chin, and his expensive, midnight blue coat was smothered with dust, suggesting a headlong ride thither.

'Her husband. Yes, I heard she — I still cannot believe it.'

'Shall I ask him to come down and speak to you, sir?'

'What? Who?' Her voice seemed to jolt him. 'No, don't bother him. I wouldn't know what to say.' He turned as if to go, but after a single irresolute step, turned back. 'If you have a chance to speak to her, will you tell her I was here?'

'Yes, sir, if that's what you want.'

'Tell her — tell her I'm sorry about everything. You will remember? It's important.'

The landlady curtsied, but she glanced around the taproom, sensing that she was needed elsewhere and more than a little annoyed at being detained.

'And tell her — no, that's all. I must go. Oh — ' He turned back one last time. 'If her condition worsens, you will send someone to tell me?'

She curtsied somewhat impatiently, but the stranger seemed not to notice her mood. He thanked her and clapped on his tricorn as he ducked through the door. The landlady bustled away, her tongue lashing a barmaid for flirting with the customers at one table, while others were left waiting. Andrew barely hesitated before he followed her.

'I won't take a moment of your time,' he said. 'The gentleman who just left, who is he?'

The landlady looked blank, her mind having already switched to her other subjects.

'You were just talking to him, the man in the blue coat.'

'Oh, you must mean Mr Ward. He's the nephew of old Mrs Ward up at t' Grange.'

He had heard the name before, but he could not place it. And then he remembered Jessica. He was tempted to demand what right Ward had to ask after Leah in that agitated manner. But pride prevented him. He couldn't help suspecting that anything he said to the landlady would quickly be passed round her customers. No-one must ever guess how little he knew about his wife's past.

'Andrew?' Leah called from behind the bed curtains as he entered.

'Yes?'

'Thank goodness. Where have you been? When I woke up and you weren't here, I didn't know what to think.' She sounded relieved and exasperated at the same time and he longed to fly across the room to her. And yet he held back.

He stopped at the foot of the bed and drew the curtain aside. Leah looked very young in her nightcap. Through her nightgown, he could see the bulge of the bandage. Should he confront her with a recital of her half-wakeful words and the scene he had just witnessed downstairs?

'Andrew?'

He realised he had been silent too

long. He could not even remember what her last words had been. He uttered a stiff laugh.

'I'm sorry. I — I needed a breath of air.'

She accepted his explanation without question. 'I hope you feel better for it. Now, don't I even merit a kiss?'

She drew him towards her with her smile. But as his lips touched hers, he heard her anguished cry. *Jack, Jack, how could you do this to me?* The words echoed in his head as he gazed at her face, hoping to gain some insight from her expression.

'What is it, Andrew?'

He hesitated before he spoke. 'Do you remember the nightmare you had earlier?'

'Nightmare? No.' Leah looked puzzled.

'You seemed to wake up and you talked about — about Jack.'

She flinched at the last word and her frown only deepened.

'I don't remember,' she said. 'Did I say anything — strange?'

Was she afraid she had revealed something incriminating? He couldn't tell. She covered her eyes with her hand as if the light made her head ache.

'Um, no,' he replied. 'Nothing coherent at any rate.'

Relief flowed visibly through her body as she sank into her pillows. He knew she was not well enough for a confrontation. And maybe he was a coward. Maybe he didn't want to know the truth. Because now he knew she was hiding something.

★ ★ ★

'Mr Melbury.' Jessica stumbled over the name as she scanned his face for hints about his news. 'It's good of you to come so early. Leah is no worse, I hope?'

'No, no, she is improving slowly and hopes you will visit her later,' Andrew replied. 'And since we are so nearly related, I suppose you'd better call me Andrew.'

'Thank you. It's so awkward, not knowing how to address you.'

'Quite.' He smiled sympathetically, then glanced at her hat and gloves. 'I see you were on your way out. Please, don't let me detain you.'

'Oh, I wasn't going anywhere in particular. Perhaps I could show you the garden?'

Andrew assented. They walked in silence with the awkwardness of strangers who knew they ought to be friends.

It had been Leah's suggestion that he should call at the parsonage after breakfast to mend the breach with her family. He was relieved to find only Jessica at home, however, and couldn't help wondering if Leah had had a fair idea that at this hour her father would be out on parish business.

'I still find it impossible to imagine that Leah is married,' Jessica began. 'She hardly mentioned you in her letters.'

Andrew suppressed a pang at her words.

'It's so out of character,' she went on. 'I've always been the impulsive one. I think Papa expects me to elope with someone totally unsuitable.'

Andrew laughed softly. 'Leah warned me when I proposed that I hardly knew her. It's only now that I am beginning to discover how true that is.'

Jessica shrugged. 'Not much to know. We lead a dull enough life here.' She gestured at the primly symmetrical garden and pulled a rueful face that reminded him of Leah. 'That's why I was so annoyed when Leah refused to marry John Ward.'

The name made him jolt.

'John Ward?' he repeated. 'A young fellow with fairish hair and an expensive taste in clothes?'

Jessica gurgled with laughter. 'Yes, that's right. Have you met him?'

'No, not as such. He asked after Leah last night.'

'Ah, I'm not surprised. He was very fond of Leah at one time.'

'But she did not return his affection?'

Andrew suggested.

Jessica's reaction took him by surprise. 'Whatever gave you that idea?'

A cold hand crept round Andrew's heart. 'Leah led me to believe that her father attempted to force her into a prudent match against her will. I assumed she meant with Mr Ward, but I see I was mistaken.'

'Oh, no, that much is true. I've never really understood the ins and outs of it. I was only a child at the time, but . . . How odd Leah didn't tell you about it herself.'

Andrew flushed under her curious gaze and murmured something incoherent.

'It would have been such an opportunity for a dowerless girl like her,' Jessica went on as if he hadn't spoken, 'and for me, I don't deny it. If Leah had married so far above her expectations, we were almost certain Papa would let her take me with her to London and Bath.'

But despite her jaunty tone, there was a wistful look in Jessica's eyes.

'Tell me about John Ward,' Andrew said.

'He's the nephew of the owner of Framworth Grange, and heir apparent too. Such an amiable man — he never ignored me, even though I was barely fourteen and quite beneath his notice. If I'd been a few years older . . . ' She sighed.

'This was some time ago?'

He must not get carried away. John — or Jack — was the most common name there was, he told himself. And was it likely that such a fine gentleman with all his prospects should become a gentleman of the road?

'Four years, though it feels longer. He and Leah were inseparable for a time. He would call at the parsonage and invite us for long walks or take us for drives in his curricle and he would always, always partner Leah at the Nottingham Assembly. Everybody spoke of it as a match, though I know there were spiteful whispers that Leah wasn't grand enough or beautiful enough and that he only paid her so much attention because she was the only young lady within walking distance of the Grange.'

'How do you know this?' Andrew asked, suspecting she had let her imagination run wild.

Jessica blushed. 'Didn't I tell you? No-one ever notices where children are or what they overhear. I didn't listen at any doors.'

'No, of course not. I didn't mean to imply . . . ' He deemed it safer to change the subject. 'So did the scoundrel raise all this gossip and then refuse to make an offer?'

'That's what's so odd. I know he spoke to Papa, because he, Papa, I mean, behaved so portentously at dinner one day after they'd been closeted in the study for an hour or more. He kept dropping what he thought were sly hints while Ward gazed at Leah's bowed head across the table.

'She'd been strange for a while, I suppose. I used to tease her about Ward and at first she blushed and giggled, but in the last weeks before the proposal she had abstracted fits. If it had been me, I would have been deliriously happy, but you see, we were all so used to Leah's being the quiet one. Papa even praised her for not allowing anything to turn her head and that sort of thing.'

Jessica frowned and said no more until Andrew felt obliged to prompt her.

'So what happened between Leah and Ward?'

'I'm not sure. Papa made certain they had an opportunity to talk. He sent them out here to admire that — ' She gestured towards a rosebush full of overblown blossom. 'It had been newly planted and there was nothing to see, except a leaf here and a thorn there, but I don't believe he could think of a better excuse. He and I sat in the parlour and he tried catechising me on my lessons, only we were both distracted and I know he glanced out of the window as many times as I did and forgot what he was saying mid-sentence.'

Andrew squirmed. All this detail would have amused him if he had not been so impatient to hear the outcome.

'I saw them standing close together, face to face. I'm pretty sure Ward was holding her hand and she didn't struggle. In fact, she didn't seem to do very much at all, except chew her lip.'

Her words conjured up images of his own proposal. Then, too, Leah had avoided his gaze while he held her hands captive. Had she been remembering this other proposal, this missed opportunity?

'Then she pulled away and several minutes elapsed before we heard the door. I expected them to enter hand-in-hand so Ward could announce the news. Instead Leah rushed upstairs and Ward came into the parlour alone. He looked — uncomfortable. He nodded to me and asked to speak to my father, so I went to talk to Leah, but she wouldn't open the bedroom door, which I thought was a bit unfair seeing as it was my room too.

'After a while, I began to feel foolish and bored, stuck on the landing like that, and I hoped Papa and Ward had had their say, so I came downstairs. I was only just in time. Ward was bidding Papa farewell and he kissed me on the forehead, something he'd never done before, so I thought things were bound to come right in the end. Papa seemed a bit put out and I badgered him until he told me that Leah hadn't refused, but had asked for a little time for consideration, which was all very proper and ladylike, but still I could see he thought that this once Leah might have dispensed with such formality.'

'So what happened next?' Andrew asked.

'Ward called every day and sometimes even I could see Leah was wavering in his favour. But then they went to the Assembly and they must have quarrelled because Leah looked so ill when she returned. She'd hardly said a word to Papa coming back, but in the end she couldn't help herself and in the privacy of our room, she confided in me for the first time.'

'What did she tell you?'

For an agonisingly long moment, Jessica stared at the gravel path.

'The first thing she said was that she didn't know how she would face Papa, but it was all over between her and John Ward. I asked her why and she said she had her reasons, but I wasn't to ask. Naturally I ignored her injunction, for all the good it did me. I asked if she loved him and she admitted that she did, but he'd broken some promise that I was too young to understand.

'I thought it would blow over quickly. Papa did everything he could to force Leah to reconsider. You have to understand she was always his favourite, being so much better behaved than I. That's why he was so angry when she said she had doubts and objections, but wouldn't say any more than that. Malicious gossip leaked out after Ward returned to London and Papa told Leah she was the author of her own misfortunes, so she took the first post she was offered as a lady's companion.'

A long pause followed the end of Jessica's narrative. Andrew listened vaguely to the sparrows chirping and rustling in the ivy on the wall. Instead of clearing his mind, this had only added to his doubts.

The possibility that Leah might have accepted him because she regretted turning down an earlier, equally lucrative match tormented him. Did she harbour a lingering affection for her first love? Did she regret the rash decision to turn Ward down because of a broken promise? Andrew knew how silly the expectations of idealistic girls could be. If Leah had come home unmarried, she would have found Ward there waiting for her.

'It's such a coincidence Ward has returned now, the first time he has visited his aunt in years,' Jessica went on, two frown marks appearing between her gracefully arched brows. 'A very odd woman, Mrs Ward. She hoards her money, despite being so rich, and sometimes she behaves as if she'll only leave her fortune to the relative who can prove he needs it least. And if what they say about John Ward is true . . . '

'You said he was a good catch.' Andrew couldn't help wondering how Ward's income compared with his own.

'Oh yes. All the old tabbies profess to be scandalised by the tales of his extravagance, while secretly wishing they too could afford to lose a thousand pounds at cards in a single night. Besides which,' Jessica added judiciously, 'the stories are bound to have become exaggerated in the retelling.'

Andrew murmured an agreement, though the mention of cards had set him thinking in another direction.

Without warning Jessica lifted her head and glanced towards the house. Belatedly Andrew remembered hearing the thud of the door and, following her gaze, he caught sight of Mr Barrowcliff hurrying along the path as fast as his portly figure would allow.

'Ah, Melbury,' he panted. 'Glad I found you. I was sent here from the Swan. There's been a development.'

7

'If you've no objections, I'll sit myself down.' Mr Barrowcliff turned to Jessica, his hand on his heart in what superficially looked like a gallant gesture, but in reality was intended to ease his breathing.

'By all means.' Jessica led the way towards a bench. 'Would you care to be left alone, or — ' Her drawl showed how anxious she was to stay.

'No, no, I wouldn't wish to drive you out of your own garden.' Mr Barrowcliff fumbled in the capacious pocket of his frockcoat for a handkerchief to mop his brow.

Andrew's impatience got the better of him. 'You said you had news.'

'Ah, yes, well. Not perhaps new, so much as — ' The older man tucked the handkerchief away with what seemed like excessive ceremony, until Andrew realised that at the same time the magistrate had extracted another object wrapped in paper.

'You've found something?'

'In a manner of speaking. This morning, while I was talking to another gentleman outside the Swan, an urchin barged past us and dropped this at my feet.'

As he spoke, Mr Barrowcliff folded back the crumpled paper to reveal something long and flexible made of cream silk thread. It jangled as he took it by one end to display a netted purse.

'It's Leah's.'

Andrew and Jessica spoke simultaneously and the latter giggled nervously.

'I was hoping you'd say that,' Mr Barrowcliff said. 'Because, unless the highwayman has an accomplice, this means he's still somewhere nearby.

Blood beating in his ears, Andrew held out his hand. 'May I?'

The magistrate nodded. Andrew fumbled with the drawstring and emptied the purse into his palm. Copper, silver, even the odd gold coin.

Nothing seemed to have been taken.

He smiled wryly. 'I don't suppose there's any sign of my pocketbook, similarly untouched?'

'I'm afraid not.'

It was only Leah he spared. What did it mean? That he could not bring himself to keep the money of the woman he had nearly killed? Or was there something more?

'Have you told my wife?'

'I thought after what happened yesterday it might be best if you did.'

Andrew nodded distractedly. He tipped the coins back into the purse and examined the paper in which it had been wrapped. Mr Barrowcliff's name was printed on it in black ink and the impression in the wax seemed to be the head of George III, indicating a coin had been used instead of a more conventional seal.

'Did you recognise the messenger?' Jessica asked.

'Can't say for sure. It was all over in a flash. I thought it might have been young Billy Carver, a scamp if there ever was one, but Ward thought not.'

'Ward?' Andrew's senses were sharpened instantly.

'Aye, he was the gentleman who was with me. He'd stopped me to ask if there was any news and to offer his services if he could help in any way.'

The cunning devil. By being present when the purse was returned, Ward could make sure it reached the right person and distract attention from the messenger.

But he is rich, Andrew chided himself. Why should he rob us? Even if he has gambling debts . . . There must be some other explanation. Why would a common thief return Leah's purse? It would have been far safer to empty it and drop it in a dark alley. And whom would Leah protect?

Mr Barrowcliff hauled himself to his feet. 'I think we've imposed on you long enough, Miss Hancock. I'll accompany you back to the inn, sir, if you've no objection.'

Andrew would have preferred to be

alone with his thoughts, but could hardly refuse. He scarcely listened to Mr Barrowcliff's condolences as they trudged along, until a familiar name struck his ear.

'Poor Ward looked as if he hadn't slept all night.' Mr Barrowcliff cleared his throat awkwardly. 'I suppose you know there was some tale before Miss Hancock went away that she and Jack Ward might, er, make a match of it?'

'So I heard.'

'Ah, well. Most likely nothing in it, just boy-and-girl nonsense, but folks like to talk.'

Andrew mustered a smile, but words were beyond him.

'A good-natured fellow,' Mr Barrowcliff went on. 'I don't know that there's a single person that doesn't like him. Free enough with his purse too. When the news came of Howe's victory at Brooklyn Heights, he insisted on treating everyone at the Swan.'

For the first time, Andrew acknowledged to himself how difficult it would be to prove Ward was guilty, if indeed he was the highwayman. If Leah would not testify against him and everyone liked him so much, nobody would want to believe it.

'He dined with me on the night of the robbery, I mind,' the squire added meditatively. 'Shame he was called away so early.'

'Called away?' Andrew echoed.

Where was Ward on the night Leah was shot? Was it significant? Dear God, don't let me get ahead of myself. There may be a perfectly rational explanation . . .

'Summoned home by a note from his aunt. Always thinking she's at death's door, Mrs Ward,' Mr Barrowcliff said with a shake of the head and an indulgent smile.

Their ways parted in the market-place. Andrew watched the portly figure trudge away before he entered the inn.

'I heard Mr Barrowcliff was looking for you,' Leah said, as he came into the room. 'Did he catch up with you?'

'Yes, he did.' He sat down on the edge of the bed so he could watch her. She was wan and heavy-eyed, lines of pain etched round her mouth.

'And?'

'It seems our thief has a conscience.'

He saw the flicker of uncertainty in her eyes. Did she perhaps wonder for a moment if the guilty man had come forward and confessed? Andrew had left the wrapping paper with the magistrate, but he took the purse out of his pocket and placed it in Leah's hand.

'Oh,' she gasped, staring at it as if it were a snake.

'Of course, I don't know how much money was in it, but if anything it is missing, it's not obvious to me.'

She made no attempt to unfasten the purse or examine its contents.

'What about you? Was nothing else — where was this found?'

Andrew explained as much as he knew and watched her lashes quiver as she listened. He wanted to confront her with his suspicions. But if he was wrong, would Leah forgive him for accusing an old friend? What proof did he have of Ward's guilt?

Only the coincidence of the first name, the possibility that Leah was shielding her assailant, the return of the purse with the money intact . . .

He stirred as if about to rise and Leah caught him by the wrist.

'Keep it,' she said, forcing the purse into his hand. 'You'll need it to pay our bills.'

★ ★ ★

Concealing his suspicions from Leah was the hardest thing Andrew had ever done. The hours crept by, with only a brief, stilted visit from Mr Hancock, a professional call from the doctor and an indifferently cooked dinner to punctuate the monotony. Jessica's arrival in the afternoon came as a welcome relief.

'To think I believed myself the most miserable creature on earth the day before you were shot,' she said, stooping to kiss her sister. 'I didn't know what real sorrow was.'

'You mustn't blame yourself,' Leah replied. 'No-one could have predicted this.'

'Even so — ' She rubbed her nose ruefully and sighed. 'It seems to trivial now.'

'What made you so unhappy?' Andrew asked, chiefly to make conversation.

'It was the first assembly of the season,' Jessica explained, 'and I was so looking forward to it. Mr Ward had made me promise in advance that I wouldn't engage myself to dance the country dances with anyone but himself.'

'I trust he was not ungentlemanly enough to disappoint you?' Andrew managed to keep his tone light, though he couldn't help noticing the glance Jessica threw at her sister as she uttered Ward's name. A twinge crossed Leah's face, but she said nothing.

'Oh, he arrived as promised and

seemed quite his usual self for the first dance or so, but then in the middle of *Admiral Rodney's Delight*, he stopped dead and turned so white, I couldn't help asking if he'd seen a ghost.'

'And what did he have to say to that?'

Jessica laughed. 'He forced a smile to his lips and said he believed I was right. Even so it was all I could do to push and pull him through the remainder of the figure and while we were standing out at the foot of the set, his gaze kept drifting. Naturally I assumed he was looking at some prettier lady, so in a pique I turned to look. But there was no-one there apart from a gentleman standing with his back to the wall.'

Unexpectedly Jessica shivered. 'I'd noticed him earlier in the evening, because he seemed to be on his own. A glowering, sinister sort of man, for all he was dressed so genteelly. He seemed quite uncomfortable in the ballroom. Mrs Barrowcliff, she was chaperoning me that night, told me later she saw him prowl about the card room like a wolf. But just as I was about to ask Ward who he was, he had to start dancing again.'

Jessica paused long enough to snatch a breath. 'We scrambled through the rest of the dance and then Ward asked if I would excuse him as he had some business to discuss. Of course I said I would. He left me seated on a bench with a glass of lemonade and I spent the rest of the evening merely looking on because all the dancing gentlemen already had partners and the rest had slunk off to the card tables. I might as well have stayed at home.'

'I find it hard to believe any man could treat you so shabbily,' Andrew remarked.

'I was quite determined never to forgive him and to make sure I always had a partner before he arrived so I could flaunt it in his face. I wouldn't even receive him when he called the next day to make his excuses and he was forced to waylay me in the street when I went to visit some of Papa's parishioners.'

'What possible excuse could he offer for his delinquency?'

'Oh, he was very abject in his apologies. Apparently an acquaintance had come all the way from London to see him, but the news was far graver than he anticipated.'

'And did you believe his story and forgive him?'

Jessica put on her primmest expression, but Andrew was not deceived. Her flushed cheeks suggested she liked John Ward too well to be implacable.

'Of course I forgave him — in the end,' she replied. 'It was the Christian thing to do.'

Leah had listened to the long narrative in silence. She kept her eyes averted and seemed unaware that Andrew had observed her throughout. He felt as if he was watching a vast panorama on a changeable day. Clouds and flashes of sunlight flitted across her face in rapid succession. But he could not guess what she was thinking.

'Perhaps the incident at the Assembly

is a — sign or a warning you should pay heed to,' she suggested, hesitating over every word.

Andrew's heartbeat quickened. Was this a confirmation of his suspicions?

'What do you mean?' Jessica stared at her sister, frankly baffled.

'I mean, I mean,' Leah's glance flickered towards her husband, 'maybe Ward has secrets nobody knows about and until he explains himself . . . '

'Why on earth should John Ward explain himself to me?' Jessica flushed crimson and her tone grew sharp.

'Oh, I know you like him and hope something might come of it. There's no point in denying it. And he is a likeable man, but — but he's not always been terribly steady.' Her voice trailed away.

Jessica had drawn herself up to her full height. 'He was steady enough in his wish to marry you,' she replied. 'It strikes me he was not the one toying with another person's affections in that instance.'

Andrew felt as if he was eavesdropping on a conversation not meant for his ears. He coughed discreetly, but it made no difference.

'Papa approves of Mr Ward,' Jessica added triumphantly, obviously pleased that for once she was the one in her father's good books.

Leah turned her face away, but not quickly enough. Andrew saw the sorrow in her eyes that had haunted her ever since the robbery.

'Papa does not know him as well as I do.' The words were uttered so softly, Andrew suspected that Jessica did not catch them.

'I can't understand why you are so unkind about Ward when he never says a word against you. He stopped me in the street on my way here to ask after you.' Her expression darkened, but still she persisted. 'Fair's fair, Leah. You already have a wealthy husband. Would you begrudge me one too, just because the same man made you an offer first?'

'No,' Leah exclaimed, catching hold

of Andrew's hand. 'I love my husband and wouldn't wish for any other. But even apparently rich men are sometimes obliged to marry heiresses. I'd hate to see you get hurt. Promise me you'll be careful.'

Andrew could feel his emotions churning inside him. He wanted to believe that Leah was telling the truth. But her hand was clammy with cold sweat and she would not look him in the eye.

'Have you ever known me to be careful in my life?' Jessica rolled her eyes.

Leah smiled back sadly. 'Don't you see that's exactly why I am so afraid for you?'

Jessica did not stay long after that. They chattered a little about less controversial topics, but Leah seemed tired and Andrew deemed it better that she should rest. Since Jessica had come accompanied only by a maid, he seized the opportunity to escort her to the parsonage.

'I'm sorry for what I said earlier,'

Jessica began. 'About Leah being jealous, I mean. It was thoughtless and tactless of me and of course she loves you best . . . '

Andrew offered her arm, but it took all his self-control to reply calmly. 'It doesn't matter.'

'Papa's always telling me to think before I speak,' Jessica went on. 'I suppose I'm a little afraid that John Ward likes Leah better than — oh!' Without warning, she stopped dead, her eyes fixed on the opposite side of the marketplace.

'What is it?' Andrew asked.

'It's him,' she hissed, clutching his arm.

'Who?'

He glanced around, but there were several men weaving between the market stalls or standing about in groups.

'The man at the Assembly,' Jessica nodded vaguely to one side, too well brought up to point. 'You know, the sinister stranger who was looking for Ward.'

Andrew turned, but barely glimpsed the swish of a black frockcoat and a booted foot as the man vanished round a corner.

'I wonder . . . ' Jessica began as Andrew steered her past a pile of market refuse.

'What now?'

'It's only — I'd forgotten about it, what with all that has happened since then, but — but I saw him in Framworth on the day Leah was shot. I remember it because I'd just forgiven Ward for deserting me at the Assembly and when I got home your letter announcing the wedding had arrived and Papa was . . . agitated.'

'Oh?' The sighting seemed of no great importance to Andrew and he was merely trying to be polite.

'You don't suppose he could be the highwayman?'

'It's not impossible, I suppose,' Andrew replied, feeling that it was highly unlikely. If this man was a stranger to Jessica, was it probable that Leah knew him?

8

A high wind picked up after dark. It wheezed in the chimney and rattled the diamond-paned windows. Andrew passed another broken night, wrestling with the information he had gathered during the day.

Leah's father had not tried to coerce her into a loveless marriage. The man she was most likely to call by his first name and want to shield was apparently too wealthy and well liked to be a common thief. And yet Leah was clearly uneasy about his friendship with her sister.

And what about the sinister stranger who seemed to be following Ward? Andrew had kept his eyes open for him on his way back from the parsonage, but to no avail. Even if he had managed to identify the man in black, what was he supposed to say? He could hardly go up to a stranger and ask him if he knew anything to John Ward's detriment without giving some explanation.

He woke much later than he had intended. Stunned by lack of sleep, he could hardly remember what was real and what he had imagined. Only one fragment of his last dream lodged in his memory. He had gone to see Ward, shouted at him, launched himself at him with his bare fists.

Perhaps he should seek Ward out. He could wrestle a confession out of him or . . . He scarcely knew what he wanted. Only that he must see the man face to face, hear his voice, try to discover what it was that Leah had seen or heard that had enabled her to identify her attacker with nothing but moonlight to assist her.

He could feel Leah watching him while he dressed and shaved, but she waited until he had dismissed his valet before she spoke.

'You're not going out so soon?' she asked as he sat down to tug on his boots.

'I'm afraid I must.'

'But you haven't had any breakfast.'

'I'm not hungry.'

'You'll waste away to a shadow.'

'I'm not hungry!' His voice rose in spite of himself.

Silence echoed.

'I'm sorry. I didn't mean to shout,' he muttered, but turned aside to pick up his hat.

'What is it, Andrew? You haven't been yourself since last night. Have I done something to offend you?'

'No.' He could not bring himself to say anything more.

'That's not true, is it? You can hardly stand to be in the same room as me any more. You can't even look at me.'

He looked at her then and saw how fragile she seemed, how easily broken. He wanted to take her home and keep her safe. But would he be imprisoning a wild bird in a cage of gold?

'Do you love me at all? Even the tiniest bit?' he asked and suddenly felt nauseous, remembering that conversation in the coach. He had thought it was all a joke then.

'Of course I love you. I would not have married you if I did not.'

There was not a flicker, not a twitch that might have betrayed uncertainty. Andrew wavered and came two steps closer. And then he remembered.

'Why didn't you tell me about Jack?'

She flushed. 'Jack?'

'Yes, Jack Ward. Why did you tell me your father tried to force you into a loveless marriage, when that patently isn't true?'

'That's not quite what I said, if you remember.'

'But it's what you implied, isn't it?'

She did not deny it.

'Do you still love him?' Now the words were out in the open, Andrew would have given anything to take them back.

'No!' Leah cried out too sharply, then moderated her voice. 'That was a long time ago. You shouldn't listen to Jessica's nonsense.'

'Is it nonsense? Then why do you cry

out his name in your sleep? Why are you protecting him? He was the one who shot you, wasn't he?'

'N-no.' But her voice trembled and he knew it was a lie.

'I'm afraid, darling, I don't believe you.'

He ran down the stairs and out into the street, desperate to put as much distance between himself and Leah as he could.

He strode at random, past the church and out into the countryside, stopping only when he was exhausted from battling against the wind. Across the expanse of recently harrowed fields, he could see the slate roof of an imposing house against the green and gold tapestry of the forest. He remembered that the Grange was somewhere outside the town, within walking distance of the parsonage. Was this the house Ward stood to inherit and which, in other circumstances, might have become Leah's home?

As if under a spell, Andrew found

himself drawn towards it. He scarcely noticed two voices, carried in snatches on the wind. Both were masculine, though one was much deeper than the other.

He caught sight of the speakers as he rounded a curve in the drive. A man in a blue coat was standing with his back towards an ancient oak, subtly pinned against its trunk by a man in black and the bay horse he was holding by the reins. The air of menace struck Andrew like ice, though both were speaking in quiet, reasonable tones.

'I swear you'll be paid in full by the end of the week.'

'You'd better see that I am, or I can't answer for the consequences.'

Andrew faltered and his foot scuffed the ground. Two faces turned towards him. The man in black hauled himself into his saddle, nodded to his companion and wheeled his horse about. He passed so close to Andrew, he could smell warm horseflesh.

Andrew was half-inclined to retreat.

But the man in the blue coat forced a genial smile to his lips and came forward a few steps.

'Is there anything I can do for you, sir?'

He doesn't know who I am, Andrew thought with a shock. He had identified Ward at a glance and somehow he had assumed recognition would be mutual.

He was younger than Andrew had realised from his earlier glimpse, with the jaded look of a schoolboy who had been dragged out of bed too early. His frockcoat was plain, though fashionably cut, the lace ruffles at his wrists and throat of high quality.

'Mr Ward?' Andrew proffered his hand. 'I'm Andrew Melbury.'

He saw the other man's Adam's apple rise as he swallowed and the realisation that Ward was as tense as he was served to settle his nerves.

'Leah Hancock's husband,' Ward said, hollowly. 'It's good of you to come. How is she? She's not — ?'

Sudden fear was audible in his voice.

'She's still alive.'

'Thank God for that.'

I know you shot her. I know you robbed us. Andrew choked down the words and fought hard to remember that terrible night. What was it that Leah had seen or heard? A scar, the flash of a gold tooth, a lisp, an unusual turn of phrase? Whatever it was, it eluded Andrew.

'It was good of you to come,' Ward repeated. 'I suppose you've heard that your wife and I were — old friends.'

A little more than that, I think. 'Oh yes, I've heard a great deal about you.'

Ward shrugged. 'Probably half of it is untrue.'

'Probably,' Andrew agreed. 'But the question is, which half?'

Ward gave him a sharp look and Andrew pulled himself up short. He must not show his hand yet. He didn't want Ward to flee before he could assemble enough evidence against him.

'I hope I didn't interrupt anything.' Andrew glanced over his shoulder, though the rider was no longer in sight.

'We'd just finished. Tell me, is there any news about the highwayman?'

Ward stumbled over his words in his haste to change the subject. Andrew's suspicions, roused by the snatch of dialogue he had overheard, were confirmed. For all his expensive gestures and great expectations, Ward was in debt, perhaps in deep financial difficulty, though it did not do to make rash assumptions.

'I believe Mr Barrowcliff has been questioning witnesses,' Andrew replied.

'Witnesses?' Ward looked confused.

'To yesterday's incident. I gather you were present when Leah's purse was returned.'

Branches creaked and shadows danced across Ward's face.

'Oh. Oh, yes. I'm sorry I couldn't be of more use. I — I suppose if you found the boy and persuaded him to talk . . . '

Suddenly there was a sharp crack above them. Andrew jerked his head up, but somehow he already knew what was happening. He had the indistinct impression of something lichen-mottled and twisted hurtling towards them, crashing through the lower branches. Then he had snatched Ward by the arm and was dragging him away.

The broken bough landed with a thud and a bounce on the exact spot where they had been standing a moment previously. Andrew felt a rush of fear there had been no time for earlier. As he released the other man's arm, he saw how pale his rival had grown.

'You — you saved my life,' Ward stammered.

'Nonsense,' Andrew replied brusquely, but his gaze was drawn back to the bough. Perhaps it was not big enough to kill one or both of them, but it would certainly have caused injuries. 'It was purely instinctive.'

'I'm grateful anyway.' Ward closed his eyes and his features twisted in agony.

'You're not hurt, are you?'

The younger man uttered a shaky laugh. 'It's nothing. I bruised my shoulder a few days ago and it's still sore, that's all.' Gingerly he rubbed his arm. 'I think perhaps we'd better go to the house. I don't know about you, but I could do with a stiff drink, or failing that, a dish of tea.'

Andrew concurred. Ward was beginning to recover his colour by the time they reached the house and he asked Andrew to say nothing about the accident to his aunt.

'She's inclined to fuss at the best of times and I don't want to upset her.'

Ward led the way into a gloomy hall and an equally gloomy drawing room. He seemed completely misplaced in his surroundings.

The room seemed to dwarf the frail-looking lady huddled close to the meagre fire. Ward stooped to kiss her wrinkled cheek, then stepped aside to introduce Andrew.

'Melbury?' she quavered. 'Melbury? I don't think I — '

'Leah Hancock's husband,' Andrew explained.

'Leah — oh, that little minx.' The corners of her mouth drooped amid folds of sagging skin.

The epithet made Andrew flinch. Ward murmured a protest and turned aside to conceal his embarrassment.

'She broke my Jack's heart,' the old lady went on querulously. 'Stole it and broke it, as if it were mere trash.'

'Now, now, Auntie, it was not so bad as that,' Ward intervened, trying hard to smile, but avoiding Andrew's eye.

'No? Then why haven't you been back to see me all these years? Even when I wrote and told you she was gone and I was sick and wanted you.'

'I told you, Auntie, it was nothing to do with that. I've been busy, that's all.'

The old lady sniffed, but looked unconvinced.

'Indeed,' Ward hurried on, to avoid prolonging the subject, 'I may have to leave again soon.'

That brought a wail of protest from

Mrs Ward and an appeal to Andrew whether she did not deserve something more than a fortnight's visit after years of neglect.

'When I think of all the love I've lavished on this thankless boy, when there are dozens of distant relatives who visit me more frequently and would be glad of a legacy . . . I've a good mind to change my Will.'

'That is your prerogative,' Ward replied, but his smile looked unsteady. 'But if you really wish it, perhaps I can put off my — engagements a little longer.'

Witnessing such a private scene embarrassed Andrew. He couldn't help feeling sorry for Ward. He had always known his grandmother was difficult. But at least she did not whine in that grating manner and had an acidic sense of humour when she was in the right mood.

Eventually the tea arrived, Mrs Ward deeming it too early for anything stronger. Ward tried to turn the conversation to more general subjects, but the highwayman seemed to fascinate his aunt.

'It's terrible what the world is coming to,' Mrs Ward shook her head. 'Such things would never have happened when I was young. I tell Jack it isn't safe to go gallivanting about like he does, but will he listen to me? Always returning home at some ungodly hour when decent folk are a-bed.'

'I very much doubt the fellow is still in the area,' Ward said with an uneasy laugh.

'It would certainly be reckless to stay close with a charge of attempted murder hanging over his head,' Andrew replied and hated himself when Ward squirmed.

Suddenly it was all too much for Andrew. He rose, using Leah as a pretext to leave.

'I'd better go too,' Ward said, rising likewise. 'Matter of business,' he added when his aunt protested. He pulled a long face. 'Terribly boring, but necessary, I'm afraid. And I'd better take a look at Shadow before I go — he still isn't fit and Harry's been badgering me about him for days.'

He waited till they were outside before he asked, 'I don't suppose you know anything about horseflesh, do you, Melbury?'

'As much as the next man, I suppose.'

'I'd appreciate an independent opinion,' Ward said, guiding him towards the stable-block to one side of the house.

They had not quite reached their destination when a servant hurried after Ward with an urgent message. The sound of voices and the clatter of hooves drew Andrew through the archway into the stable-yard.

A groom was leaning against the half-door of an empty stall, hat tipped forward to shield his eyes, his hands in his pockets and a straw flicking up and down as he chewed it thoughtfully. In front of him a lad of about fourteen was leading a fine black stallion to try out its paces.

'Magnificent beast,' Andrew commented.

The groom pushed himself upright at the sound of his voice and nudged his hat further back.

'Aye, sir, that he is, though he's got a temper on him when he chooses.'

'I can imagine. Belongs to Mrs Ward, does he?'

The servant grinned and the straw, still miraculously stuck to his lower lip, danced like the tail of a wagtail.

'Nay, sir, she's no use for this sort of stallion,' he replied, nodding vaguely in the direction of the other stalls. 'Carriage horses and farm horses is all she ever makes use on, and most of them's nearly as old as she is.' He uttered a discordant laugh.

'This 'un belongs to the young master,' the groom went on, confirming what Andrew had suspected from the start.

'I don't suppose he'd be willing to sell.'

He had no intention of buying the

black stallion, but he was anxious to see how much the groom was willing to talk about his mistress's nephew.

'You suppose right. He'll never part with Shadow, though he must be upward of twelve years old. Good for his age too, I'll grant you, only the young master forgets sometimes he's not in his first flush no more.'

'He does seem rather lame,' Andrew remarked, viewing the horse with a critical eye.

'Oh, lame right enough, though nothing like as bad as he were two, three days ago.'

'Cast a shoe, did he?'

'Nah. Inflammation, that's what it is. Look here.' He ran surprisingly gentle hands down one of the horse's hind legs and lifted it to show where the muscle had swollen.

'You only get that from riding him too hard. I'll say this, though, for the young master. He insisted on taking care of Shadow himself, rubbing him down and what have you, for all it was so late and he still in his finery after supping with Squire Barrowcliff. Must've thrown him and all — his arm were that stiff and bruised, he had to give over after a time and let me finish up.'

Andrew shivered suddenly. The horse had turned its head towards him for the first time and now he saw what Leah must have seen on the night of the robbery. The white star on the stallion's forehead.

9

'There you are.' The words meant nothing to Andrew. He heard steps approaching from behind. The stallion whickered and stretched its muzzle towards its master.

'What do you think of him?' Ward asked, pride unmistakable in his voice as he laid a proprietorial hand on the horse's neck.

'A magnificent beast,' Andrew repeated his earlier words mechanically.

Could the groom by induced to tell the same story to the authorities? The master tending his overridden horse in his best clothes, the lateness of the hour though Mr Barrowcliff claimed Ward had left his house unusually early . . .

But in itself it was nothing. Would it be justifiable to lie and say he had seen the white mark Ward was caressing with his fingertips, unconscious that it might be his downfall? Was he even sure the groom was referring to the same night?

Ward was talking enthusiastically about horses, those he owned or perhaps those he had betted on. Andrew couldn't be sure which. He didn't know how long he could keep up the pretence that nothing was wrong.

'What is it? You don't look well.'

Ward's words penetrated slowly. 'It's nothing. I'm just tired, I suppose. I slept badly.'

The night of the attack came back to him, the reverberation of the shot, the nightmarish drive through the forest, terrified that Leah was bleeding to death in his arms. His valet's voice echoed in his head.

I can't be sure, but I think I hit him.

Suppose Ward's stiff shoulder was not the result of a riding accident. Suppose he had been struck by a spent bullet, which had travelled too far to penetrate the flesh, though it could still inflict a bruise.

Suddenly Andrew felt dizzy. He

allowed himself to be pushed down on to the mounting block. From a vast distance he heard Ward giving orders, but it was not till he was ushered towards an ancient coach that he realised what all the noise was about. He protested, but Ward overruled him.

'I wouldn't dream of letting you go on foot. And you'll be doing my aunt's horses a favour. It's not often they get much exercise nowadays, except to go to church.'

Andrew wavered in his assessment of Ward. Could a man who was capable of so much kindness really be a thief and a murderer?

He had hoped to think it all out in the carriage before he got back to Framworth, but Ward scrambled in after him and the coach lurched into motion as briskly as the indolent horses and ramshackle vehicle would allow.

'Thank you.' Andrew managed a pallid smile.

'It's been a difficult time for you,' Ward said with a visible effort. 'If it's any consolation, you're not the only one who has been praying for Le — Miss — that is, Mrs Melbury's recovery.'

He flushed deep red at his struggle to find the right name and dropped his head to hide his expression. But Andrew could not doubt his sincerity.

He must be wrong. He must be. The very thought made him feel better. The Jack who shot Leah was someone else, someone she had known a long time ago, but had never cared for.

The coach stopped as abruptly as it had set off and Andrew stared at his surroundings. It had seemed such a long way to the Grange in the opposite direction. He could not believe they had reached their destination already. He was about to thank Ward and offer to shake hands when the younger man spoke.

'I know it's a terrible imposition, but do you suppose Leah would agree to see me?'

Andrew noticed the use of the first name, though Ward seemed unaware of his lapse.

'It would only be for a minute,' he urged, 'and in your presence, if you prefer. I only wanted to tell her in person how very sorry I am about . . . ' His voice trailed away.

Andrew ran his hand over his forehead. 'I'll go and see how she is,' he said quietly, 'but I can promise nothing.'

His head felt light as he mounted the by now familiar stairs. As he turned the last corner, he heard hushed voices and a smothered giggle. His valet and Leah's maid were standing in unmistakably close proximity outside the door of the sickroom.

'What the devil are you doing here?' Andrew asked, not sure if he ought to be angry.

Betty swished round, alarm and guilt etched on her face. 'If you please, sir, the mistress, she said she'd some letters to write and she couldn't think straight with me fussing over her, so she said I wasn't to disturb her until she called . . . '

'I see.'

Andrew pushed open the door, but after two steps he reeled back. Leah was slumped across the rickety deal table, the quill still resting in her motionless fingers.

'Betty, Thomas, come quickly.'

He stooped over Leah to lift her. For a ghastly moment he wondered if an assassin could have found a way into the room while he was away and the servants distracted. But as his wife's head rolled back to settle against his shoulder, he felt her breath on his cheek.

She's overexerted herself and fainted, that's all, he told himself. Even so, he sent his valet to fetch the doctor while Betty scrabbled around for some hartshorn.

'How long is it since you left her? Did you hear nothing from outside the room?'

'N-no, I don't know, sir. I — I lost track of time. But if I'd heard anything I would've come to see what was wrong. Oh, I knew she wasn't strong enough to be up, but she was so restless and I didn't like to cross her . . . '

Andrew felt a pang of guilt at her words. He lifted Leah out of the only comfortable chair in the room and carried her back to the bed. She was dressed in a pale blue gown and matching petticoat, though she had left off her stays. Her eyelashes began to flutter as he laid her on the bed and she uttered a moan of pain.

'Leah, darling, can you hear me?'

Her eyes opened properly this time, though it seemed to take her a moment to recognise him. Andrew motioned to Betty to leave.

'What is it?' Leah's voice was slurred. 'What's happened?'

'You got up too soon and fainted.' The words spilled out before he could stop them. 'Oh God, Leah, this is my fault, isn't it?'

'Your fault?' she echoed.

'I shouldn't have upset you this

morning. I was jealous and unreason-able and I shouldn't have stormed off like that. Can you forgive me?'

Slowly the light of remembrance dawned in Leah's eyes. She sighed. 'Oh, Andrew, I never thought we would begin to quarrel so early in our marriage.'

'Neither did I.'

But when he stooped to kiss her, she flinched at the last moment so his lips brushed her cheek instead of her mouth. He couldn't help feeling rebuffed. Leah wouldn't even look him in the eye. She tried to hoist herself up, but her injured arm buckled beneath her.

'Lie still.'

Leah's gaze flitted uneasily towards the table. 'There's something I ought to tell you.'

Her words sent a cold tingle down his spine.

'You were right,' she went on. 'I didn't tell you the truth about my past, but it wasn't deliberate. It's just that in all the excitement and hurry of the wedding, it didn't seem important. You do understand, don't you?'

'Yes, I suppose so.' What else could he say?

Unspoken words hovered in the air. At the back of his mind, Andrew was aware of all the evidence he had gathered against Ward, flimsy though it was.

Again Leah glanced towards the table. 'It would be foolish to deny I was once in love with John Ward,' she said. 'That's why . . . '

A tap at the door interrupted her. It proved to be doctor. He did not seem the least surprised by Andrew's account of Leah's faint.

'I'm afraid that's what happens if you insist on getting up without permission,' he said, giving Leah a stern look. 'Do you want to catch an infection?'

He insisted on a thorough examination, but seemed grudgingly satisfied by the results. Then he sat down to write out his instructions.

'What's happened? Is Leah worse?'

Jessica burst into the room and bombarded them with questions until they managed to reassure her.

'Thank goodness,' she sighed. 'I own I feared the worst when Mr Ward stopped me because he assumed you must have sent for me.'

'Ward. I completely forgot he was here. I suppose I'd better go and talk to him.' In truth, Andrew was not looking forward to the interview, unsure what he ought to say.

'I'm sure he understands,' Jessica said soothingly.

But Andrew had caught sight of Leah's face. What little colour she had regained since her swoon had forsaken her and she looked disquieted.

'He shouldn't be here,' she whispered.

'I agree,' the doctor pronounced, pushing back his chair. 'It's imperative that Mrs Melbury should rest and I'll tell Mr Ward so on my way out, if you wish.'

Andrew thanked him and shook

hands with him at the door. While Jessica took leave of her sister, he wandered across to the table to glance at the doctor's scrawl.

It was only after he had picked it up that he realised he had taken the wrong note. The handwriting was agitated, quite unlike Leah's usual hand, and a large inkblot had pooled where she had dropped her pen. His eye fell unconsciously on the words and had taken them in before he realised what he was doing.

The net is closing in. If you ever had any consideration for me, or my sister, you must leave the area at once. I cannot protect you much longer. L.

★   ★   ★

Andrew wandered into the taproom. Leah was lying down, but he could not settle. He knew he must not say anything to her until he had had a

145

chance to think through the implications of the note. He had left it on the table where he found it, but every word was etched on his inner eye.

Although the note was not addressed to anyone, the reference to Jessica made it plain who the intended recipient was. Suspicions crept into Andrew's mind. What was it that Leah had wanted to tell him before the doctor arrived?

He couldn't explain why his eyes were drawn to a particular figure in the crowded taproom. It was the man he had seen threatening Ward that morning. There seemed to be a darkness about him, like the opposite of a halo. Perhaps he sensed Andrew's gaze. At any rate, the stranger raised his head and looked him straight in the eye as he approached.

'You're a friend of John Ward, I believe?' Andrew asked, adding hastily, 'I saw you with him this morning.'

'I remember,' the stranger replied in a sonorous bass. 'Henry Stoddard.'

'Andrew Melbury.'

Stoddard did not offer to shake hands so Andrew merely returned his nod. He had to play his cards carefully.

They sat in silence, only glancing at each other from the tails of their eyes, until a glass had been set before Andrew and the other man's had been replenished.

'An agreeable fellow, Ward,' Andrew ventured. 'You'd never think he could have so many secrets.'

Stoddard allowed himself something resembling an appreciative grin, though it failed to reach his eyes. 'Ah, so you've found that out. Not many do.'

Andrew felt a shiver run down his spine.

'Owes you money, does he?' Stoddard asked.

'What makes you say that?' He had not dared hope for confirmation of his suspicions so quickly.

The other man shrugged. 'He owes a lot of people money in London. Tradesmen's bills, debts of honour . . . I've made it my business to find out. And by your account, you're not from these parts.'

Andrew felt the chill sink deeper into his bones. 'I take it he owes you a considerable sum?' he suggested.

For a while he thought Stoddard was not going to reply, but his scrutiny of Andrew's face was answer enough.

'Yes,' he replied at last and took another pull from his glass. 'And if you've any friendship for Ward, perhaps you'd advise him it's not wise to keep me waiting. I'm not a patient man.'

With that Stoddard pushed back his chair. He nodded, but took no other farewell before stalking off. Andrew remained seated a while longer, staring into his glass. He needed to talk to someone. Coming to a decision, he went to see Mr Barrowcliff.

'I was about to call on you,' the magistrate said as Andrew was shown into his study. 'Not that there's much new to the case.'

So far he had failed to locate any

witness who could identify the messenger who returned Leah's purse. He had questioned Billy Carver, but the boy denied everything.

Andrew had barely enough patience to hear him out. He told Mr Barrowcliff all he had discovered, deliberately overstating his case when he saw the scepticism in the older man's eyes. The only thing he failed to mention was Leah's note.

'Nay, but Jack Ward,' the magistrate protested. 'I've known him since he were a lad.'

'What about the mark on the horse's forehead?' Andrew demanded, trying to convince himself that he had really seen it.

'It's not so very uncommon,' Mr Barrowcliff pointed out. 'And mayhap you misremembered that?'

Andrew's shoulders slumped. He appreciated the other man's tact in not accusing him outright of lying.

'I don't doubt, but you're right in saying Jack Ward has exceeded his

149

income from time to time or accumulated the odd debt,' Mr Barrowcliff went on. 'But you must remember he was bred a gentleman and he's always been so fond of Miss Hancock, I can't believe he'd ever hurt a hair on her head.'

Andrew was brought up short as he opened the door. Leah's room was in darkness. The candle that was usually kept alight in a shaded corner had obviously blown out in a draught. The scent of warm wax hung in the air.

His first thought was that Betty had fallen asleep and failed to notice the absence of light. But the chair by the bed was empty. He could hear no sound within the room, no matter how intently he strained his ears. Suppose something had happened to Leah.

It took all his nerve to draw back the bed curtains. His heart leapt in relief as Leah muttered something incoherent. But she showed no sign of waking.

Inside him anger was beginning to

boil. What business had Betty to desert her mistress? Suppose Leah had wanted something, or someone had taken advantage of the maid's absence?

Restlessly, he strode across to the window. Then he froze. There was a figure in the yard below gazing at the upper windows. As he watched, the man drew into the shadows. But Andrew had no doubt, even at this distance, that the watcher was John Ward.

He had not decided what to make of his rival's presence when he heard hasty steps outside the room. Slowly, slowly, the door creaked open and he could hear the ragged panting of someone who was trying to conceal that he or she had been running.

The beam of the candle did not reach the window and since Andrew remained motionless, the maid did not notice him.

'Mrs Melbury?' she whispered. 'Are you awake?'

Andrew took a step forward and the

floorboard groaned. Betty started and whirled in his direction. Something white fell from her fingers and she scrabbled to retrieve it.

'Oh — oh, sir, I didn't know — '

'What the devil do you mean by it, leaving your mistress unattended?' Andrew demanded in an angry whisper. He snatched her arm and dragged her out into the corridor. 'Anything might have happened in your absence.'

'I — I was only gone two minutes,' she gasped.

'I've been here longer than that.' He had no idea if this was true, but he was too angry to care.

The maid ducked her head. Part of him felt sorry for her, but he could not seem to help himself. He needed to vent his frustrations.

'I've a good mind to dismiss you without a reference,' he went on, though he was not aware of having any such intention a moment previously. As his gaze dropped lower, he noticed Betty trying to hide something beneath her apron.

'And don't fidget when I'm talking to you,' he said. Suspicion suddenly flared up inside him. 'What have you got there?'

'N-nothing.'

'Don't add to your guilt by lying. I saw the letter. Show it to me.'

'I — I can't, sir. I mustn't — I promised . . . '

'Do you want to pack your things and depart at first light? It can be arranged.'

Betty was shaking from head to foot, but she made one last attempt to resist.

Andrew made no verbal reply, but his stern look had the desired effect. When he held out his hand, the maid relinquished the letter. If it really was for her, Andrew resolved he would return it unopened. It would be a relief to know he had been mistaken about the identity of the man watching Leah's window.

He held the note closer to the light, but the letters danced. Then the paper began to shake as he made out the name.

Mrs Andrew Melbury.

10

'Where did you get this?' Andrew's voice was dangerously quiet. It was a man's handwriting on the letter, but not Mr Hancock's or Mr Barrowcliff's. Who else was left?

'A — a gentleman gave it to me.'

'A young man? Well-dressed with fair hair?'

She bobbed a nervous curtsey. 'Yes, sir. He — he said he was an old friend of Mrs Melbury and I didn't see any harm in delivering a letter for him.'

No doubt she had been well paid for the favour, but Andrew had no interest in that side of the transaction.

'Didn't he tell you the letter had to be kept a secret?'

'Yes, sir.'

'So you must have known it was wrong to take it.'

She looked up, startled. 'Oh, but

— no — that is — '

She had been dazzled by Jack Ward's winning ways, there could be no doubt about that. She was on the brink of tears even now.

'He, he seemed such, such a pleasant gentleman,' she gulped. 'I'm sorry if I've done wrong, but, but you won't send me back to Hereford, will you? My stepfather will beat me and — ' She stopped and glanced around, as if merely mentioning her stepfather might conjure him up.

Andrew let her wait, though he never wavered in his decision. 'I won't send you back — yet.' He paused to let the last word sink in. 'I'm prepared to give you another chance since you've told me the truth now. You have told me everything, haven't you?'

The maid seemed to search her memory hastily.

'Y-yes, sir. Oh, except — well, the gentleman, he said he'd be waiting at the Crown Inn if the mistress wanted to send a message.'

Andrew felt a surge of anger. Ward obviously felt confident that Leah would want to continue their correspondence.

He dismissed Betty with an injunction to stay within call in case he needed her. He didn't want her to go to Ward on her own initiative to tell him what had befallen his letter.

Andrew turned back to the sickroom, half-determined to wake Leah and give her the letter unopened. But when he pushed back the curtain, he found that for once she was sleeping soundly. Unconsciously he twisted the paper in his hands. The seal cracked and the sound echoed as loudly as a pistol shot in his ears. But Leah did not stir.

Andrew stared at the letter, fighting waves of temptation. Now it was open, wasn't he more or less committed to reading it? Even if he gave it to Leah, she would see the broken seal and perhaps would not believe that he hadn't read it. And suppose the letter contained something that might upset

Leah? Or what if Ward was trying to lure her away from him?

Andrew turned on his heel, intending to place the letter on the table, out of harm's way. Something tinkled as it struck the floor and rolled away. He snatched up the candle and its light caught the gleam of the missing earring. He clasped it tight in his fist. Now he had proof. There was nothing to stop him now. The paper crackled as he unfolded it.

Dearest Leah.

The words made Andrew see red. But he forced himself to sit down and read on.

Forgive the freedom of the address. I have no right to call you that any more, though I am all too aware that this is the least of my sins. I couldn't obey your injunction to flee without making one more attempt to see you, or at least let you know how truly sorry I am for everything that has happened.

Looking up, Andrew noticed for the first time that Leah's writing things had been cleared away and the note was gone.

I swear I never meant to hurt anyone that night. It was the first time I ever attempted such a thing and the bullet was intended merely for my own protection. I know it's no excuse, but I was desperate. My chief creditor is merciless, but I shall not complain. You always told me my love of gambling would ruin me and now it has brought me to the gallows.

Forgive me, forgive me. I never meant to hurt you — you of all people. I didn't know you in the dark and never expected to see you in this county after your long absence. When you called my name and I recognised your voice, I started. My finger was on the trigger and I was powerless to stop it when the spark ignited the powder.

So many times since then I have seen that chain of events, heard the echo of the shot and prayed to God for a chance to undo it. I have been on the brink of destroying myself several times. I even went to Mr Barrowcliff to confess, and yet at the last moment, the words would not pass my lips. I know I am weak, but in spite of everything, I find I cling tenaciously to life.

A flare of triumph lit up inside Andrew. Here is proof of Ward's guilt. You could force Barrowcliff to believe you. Everyone would see Ward for what he really is. Should he be allowed to go unpunished?

And yet the letter also revealed the extent of Ward's suffering. If, of course, it was sincere and not merely a calculated attempt to wring Leah's heart and prevent her from testifying against him.

Then on top of everything, I find you are married. I wouldn't believe it at first. For months now I have been dogged by duns and a dozen times I've wanted to ask your sister for your address, determined that I would find you and beg for your help.

Would I have been too late? I have hated Melbury with a passion from the moment I realised I had lost you forever. I even confess that I wished I had shot him instead so I could console you in your widowhood and become a reformed character. Though I doubt my conscience would have allowed me to carry out this plan.

All that is over now. I have hurt you too much already and I know you would not have married Melbury unless you loved him.

Could Ward be right? For a moment hope flared up inside Andrew and then he remembered all he had done to forfeit Leah's love. He lowered the letter, feeling sick and guilty that his jealousy had led him to violate her privacy for a second time.

Sheets rustled behind him. Curtains swished.

'Andrew? Are you there?'

It took him a moment to respond. 'Yes, I'm here.'

Two bare feet dropped to the floor. The sound made Andrew rise, crushing the letter in his fist and stuffing it into his pocket. Leah was standing beside the bed. Even from this distance, he could see she was shivering.

'You shouldn't be out of bed,' he said. He was glad the room was dark. He didn't want her to see his face until he had had time to work out what to do with the letter.

'I have to speak to you,' she said. 'I didn't intend to fall asleep, but you were gone such a long time. Where have you been?'

'I went to see Mr Barrowcliff.'

Her expression changed. She tottered forwards a few steps, snatching the bedpost for support.

'Am I too late?' she whispered. 'Did — did you tell him whom you suspect of being the highwayman?'

Her obvious distress wrung Andrew's heart. The lie was out of his mouth before he had time to think.

'No, I didn't tell him.' What did it matter? Barrowcliff had not believed him anyway.

She closed her eyes for two seconds and then suddenly he found her nestling against his breast. 'Thank you,' she murmured. 'You don't know what this means to me.'

She had struck a dagger to his heart and twisted it. Guilt and self-loathing washed over Andrew and he wondered that Leah could not hear the crackle of paper in his pocket as she pressed against him. The momentary triumph when he held Ward's confession in his hand seemed like a distant memory. If Leah cared for this man, his execution would devastate her.

She had been leaning with her cheek against his shoulder. Now she pulled away and moved towards the table.

'It's funny,' she laughed forlornly. 'All the time you were away, I was desperate to talk to you and I was so sure I would know exactly what to say. Now I don't even know where to begin.'

She stretched out her hand to pick up something small from the table. As she groped for words, she toyed with the object, passing it from one hand to the other.

'You were right about Jack Ward. But I couldn't betray him, not after everything that happened in the past.'

Andrew could feel the letter burning a hole in his pocket, searing his flesh. There was no need to spy on her, his conscience whispered. She intended to tell you all along.

'I know I've no right to ask this of you,' Leah went on, 'but I beg you to spare him. I know he did a terrible thing and you have suffered as much as I, but — '

I could give her the letter, confess what I have done.

'Leah, before you go on, there's something I should . . . ' he interrupted.

She picked up a trinket box and, with a twinge of fear, Andrew realised the object she had been toying with was the second earring. He uttered a silent prayer. Perhaps she would not notice its pair and . . . Slowly Leah turned towards him.

'Andrew?' She sounded bewildered. One golden hoop glittered in each hand between her thumb and forefinger. 'I don't understand. Where did this come from?'

It crossed his mind to tell he had had her earring copied, or that Mr Barrowcliff had found it. But there had already been too many lies between them.

'It was in this,' he said. He pulled the letter out of his pocket. Leah stared at him, her eyes wide and uncomprehending. Then the colour drained from her face.

'What is that?' she whispered.

'A letter from Ward.'

'He wrote to you?' She flushed and paled again. 'Did he — what did he say?'

Andrew hesitated. Her assumption that the letter was for him offered him a way out. But did he want to take it?

'Please, Andrew, I have a right to know.'

'It — it's tantamount to a full confession. He begs for your forgiveness and claims he pulled the trigger by mistake, being taken by surprise . . . '

He saw her relax and close her eyes momentarily. The silence echoed, filled only with sounds that drifted up from the stables and the taproom below.

'May I read it?'

Dread and guilt hit him in the stomach like a well-aimed punch.

'Please, Andrew, this concerns me as much as — ' She caught sight of his face. 'The letter wasn't for you, was it?'

He could not deny it, nor look her in the eye.

'I trusted you.' Anger was becoming more and more audible in her voice. 'How could you pry into my letters? Am I nothing but a — a possession to you?'

'Isn't that what you are?' he asked in a low tone. 'Didn't you sell yourself to me for money, while I deluded myself that you married me for love?'

For a moment her lips trembled wordlessly. 'How can you say such a thing? Don't you know me better than that?'

She had drawn away from him and was clinging to the bedpost for support, her eyes burning into his soul. In the silence, he could hear every sharp intake of her breath. A raucous laugh rose from the taproom below.

'If you are not in love with Ward, why have you been protecting him all this time?'

'Wouldn't you do the same for an old friend?'

The reasonable side of him winced. She was right. Perhaps he had read too

167

much into the situation.

'I'm sorry, Leah. I know I shouldn't have done it. I know it's no excuse, but I was afraid of losing you.'

She will never forgive me, never. Why did I begin this? He wanted to make it up to her. He wanted to prove himself worthy of her love.

Leah gave a despairing shrug and uttered an inarticulate cry.

'Here.'

He thrust the letter into her hands. What did it matter whether she destroyed it and Jack Ward escaped justice? Revenge or forbearance — neither would win back his wife, now he had made her hate him. They would lead separate lives, sleep in separate rooms, cultivate separate friends, like so many fashionable couples. A shadow would always stand between them. Ward had not killed Leah, but he had destroyed their marriage nonetheless.

The letter dropped from Leah's fingers as she sank down on the edge of the bed.

'Oh, Jack, Jack.' She uttered a crackled laugh that was almost a sob and covered her face with her hands. 'What have I done to you?'

11

Silence followed her cry of anguish. Through the floorboards, Andrew could hear a mixture of voices, the clatter of dishes, the banging of doors. The blood beat in his forehead as he sought an explanation for Leah's words.

'It's all my fault.' A tear trickled down her cheek, but she swiped it away.

Her lashes rose, glittering with tears. 'I abandoned him to his own weak character. If I had married him, perhaps I could have saved him from himself. I know his drinking and gambling grew worse after I rejected him. I might have broken him of his bad habits, kept him away from dangerous influences if I had made one more attempt. He begged me so many times to save him, but I didn't love him enough.'

Her voice broke. Powerful sobs racked her. Andrew took her in his arms and held her, despite her initial resistance. The same words kept echoing in his head as he stroked her back. I didn't love him enough.

'And now I've brought him to the foot of the gallows ... '

'No! Leah, you mustn't think that way. Nobody forced Ward to make the decisions he made, least of all you. And nobody can stop someone who is bent on self-destruction. All that would have happened is that Ward would have dragged you and any children you might have had down with him.'

'I wish I could believe you.'

Her face felt hot and feverish against his breast. Cold tears drenched his shirt. He understood now why she had been unable to betray Jack Ward.

'I'm sorry, Leah, for making things harder for you. Can you forgive me?'

He was not sure she heard him. Certainly she did not reply and he did not press the point.

There was a knock. Leah physically jumped and instinctively Andrew's arms tightened around her. Betty curtsied at the door.

'Mr Barrowcliff is here to see you, sir,' she said. 'He says he has news.'

Leah had turned her face towards the door as it opened. Now her head dropped and her eyes came to rest on the incriminating letter. But she made no attempt to pick it up or to plead with him any more. The silence stretched on and on as Andrew struggled to decide what to do.

'Tell him I'll be with him in a minute.'

As the door closed behind the maid, Leah drew herself out of Andrew's arms. He rose, hesitated, then plucked up the incriminating letter. He heard a slight sound that was maybe a suppressed sob catching the back of Leah's throat. Quickly, before he could change his mind, he held the corner of the letter in the nearest candle.

The paper flared up faster than he had expected, the flames illuminating individual words seconds before they devoured them. They scorched his fingers and he dropped the crumbling remains on to the metal base of the candlestick.

The flames died as suddenly as they had sprung up, leaving blackness at the centre of his vision. Without a word, he groped his way to the door.

'You were right, Melbury.'

Andrew froze at these opening words, but Mr Barrowcliff seemed not to notice.

'The parish constable found two witnesses who'd seen Billy Carver running outside the Swan yester morn, so I had the lad hauled back to my house.'

Andrew shivered. Only an hour ago, he might have been exultant. Now foreboding swamped him. Mr Barrowcliff looked tired and aged, but there was grim determination in the set of his lips. He might not relish the task ahead of him, but he would carry out his duty nonetheless.

'What did the boy have to say?'

Andrew could barely force the words out.

Will Leah ever forgive me if, in spite of all I have said, I am responsible for hanging a man she was once fond of and still feels responsible for?

Mr Barrowcliff uttered a grim chuckle. 'He's a clever enough lad, I'll give him that, not easily intimidated and fiercely loyal. Jack Ward chose wisely when he picked him.'

The fact that the magistrate had mentioned Ward by name sank Andrew's last hope.

'I had to trick him into betraying his master, by asking him what reward Mr Ward had offered him to keep his mouth shut. The lad flew to Ward's defence and then stopped and refused to say another word, but he knew and I knew he'd indirectly confessed.'

Andrew's mind whirred. So far the evidence amounted to very little.

'I thought you'd like to know,' the older man continued, though Andrew's unresponsiveness was beginning to make him uneasy. 'Do you reckon I should question the lad again, come the morn? Or should I go straight to the serpent's head, as it were?'

Andrew hesitated and when he replied, each word dropped out slowly, as if it had manacles attached to its ankles.

'Is there any need to proceed with this at all?'

There was an electrified silence as the eyes of the two men met.

'Oh, but the wheels of justice have been set in motion,' Mr Barrowcliff blustered unconvincingly. 'The constable and my clerk were present when I questioned the boy.'

'But the evidence is flimsy and the boy said very little.' Andrew grasped at any straw. 'You say Ward is immensely liked. How plausible is it that he could commit such a crime?'

'It's my duty to apprehend all malefactors, regardless of . . . ' His voice trailed away.

'Do you really think Ward is likely to

repeat his crime?' Andrew urged. 'He's had a terrible shock, the worst, I think, there can possibly be.'

Mr Barrowcliff stared long and hard at him. And then suddenly his shoulders slumped in relief. 'I suppose nothing is irreversible.'

Once the magistrate had departed, Andrew rang for the landlord and asked for pen, ink and paper. It was as well he had written many such letters in the past. Correct expressions and mellifluous phrases came to him without much need for forethought. He read the letter over once before sanding and folding it, though he did not seal it. Then he asked for directions to the Crown. He decided against informing Leah that he was going out. He didn't want her to worry in his absence.

It was not far to the second largest inn in Framworth. At first glance, Jack Ward appeared perfectly at home there, treating the assembled company to the best ale and his most amusing anecdotes. But as he recognised the newcomer, Andrew saw a shade of anxiety cross his features.

Try as he might, Andrew couldn't muster a smile. He was struck by how young Ward was to have thrown away all his advantages, and almost his life, in his reckless pursuit of pleasure.

'Is there anywhere we could talk privately?'

Ward paled at his grave tone, but he managed to suppress his questions until they had been shown into a small backroom that stank of spilt ale and fried onions.

'It's Leah, isn't it?' He grasped Andrew's sleeve. 'She's taken a turn for the worse.'

'No. Leah is — rather better than she was.' Andrew hesitated, choosing his words carefully. 'I came to talk to you about a different matter.'

Ward released him, but they were still very close. His eyes never left Andrew's face as he uttered the next words.

'It concerns a letter that has fallen into my possession.'

177

Ward's eyes widened as he scrutinised Andrew's face for confirmation of his darkest fear. Then abruptly, he turned away and strode across the room. He stopped by the table to stare at its surface. But still he did not speak, as if afraid of betraying something that Andrew did not already know.

'A letter,' Andrew went on, 'that is as good as a confession of your guilt.'

At that Ward spun round, desperation in his eyes.

'What do you want from me, Melbury?' he demanded. 'Have you come to gloat? Do you want reparation? Do you want me to go to Barrowcliff and confess? Would it not have been enough for you to send the parish constable to — ' He choked over his words.

'I want you to listen to me. You owe me that much at least.'

For a moment Ward held his gaze defiantly. Then he wavered and collapsed sideways into a chair.

'I would be lying if I said I hadn't

dreamt of seeing you hanged or transported. But Leah is fond of you, for old times' sake. That's why I burnt the letter.'

Trembling, Ward raised his head. Andrew couldn't bring himself to watch hope and doubt fluttering in the younger man's eyes. Instead he groped in his coat pocket for the letter he had written after Mr Barrowcliff's departure.

'Here, take this.'

Doubtfully Ward stretched out his hand. 'What is it?'

'It's addressed to my banker in London. If you call at that address, it authorises you to receive a sum of money. I've no idea how large your debts might be and I've no wish to know. I doubt a thousand pounds will cover what you owe, but it's all I can spare.'

'A thous . . . And what am I to do with this money, if I accept it?'

Andrew could not help grudgingly approve of the 'if' and the defensive tone of his companion.

'Whatever seems most prudent. Discharge the most pressing of your debts — Stoddard seems a nasty customer — or buy yourself a commission in a fashionable regiment or flee abroad. Anything other than risk it all on a game of chance.'

'You trust me with this? Or are you making sport of me?'

'I am quite serious. Read the letter yourself if you don't believe me.'

'But — you do know I have no prospect of repaying you? If my aunt should decide to leave her fortune to someone else . . . '

'I don't expect to be repaid. I think I know you well enough from what I have seen and heard of you.'

The darkness of the room could not conceal Ward's flush of annoyance and shame.

'I don't even expect you to be grateful. I hope you will learn from this experience, but I'm not going to break my heart if you prove me wrong and go straight to the devil.'

'You're not wrong,' Ward replied in a low, eager tone. 'You've no idea what purgatory I have suffered ever since . . . I want to change and lead a better life. I've wanted to for a long time, but I was sunk so deep, I couldn't see any way of getting out.'

He stopped, embarrassed at having revealed so much to a virtual stranger.

'Just remember,' Andrew said in a softened tone, 'I may not care what becomes of you, but if you did end up in a bad way, Leah would blame herself.'

He intended those to be his last words and turned to leave.

'Melbury.'

'Yes?'

'Thank you. It's more than I deserve. I've robbed you once already.'

Ward hesitantly held out his hand. Andrew smiled ruefully as he clasped it.

'I must get back to Leah,' he said. 'She doesn't know where I am.'

'Of course. But I do mean it. I am

grateful. And if I am ever in a position to repay you, I will.'

Tiredness hit Andrew like a warm wave as he entered the Swan. It was all he could do to drag his heavy limbs up the stairs. He was vaguely aware of the rustle of petticoats coming towards him along the dark corridor and he stood aside to let the women pass.

To his surprise, they stopped too. Baffled, Andrew looked properly at them for the first time. His eye fell on Betty. The other woman was half-hidden by the shadows, but he could not be mistaken about her identity.

'Leah!' he exclaimed. 'What are you doing here?'

She was fully clothed, he noted, her blue hat pulled well forward to shield her face.

'I was going to find you. I was worried. Where have you been?'

Something had upset her.

'I had some business to transact,' he replied, glancing at the maid. He did not necessarily want to reveal everything in front of her. 'You shouldn't be out of bed. The doctor — '

Leah shrugged impatiently. 'The doctor, the doctor. I'm sick of the doctor and bed and being treated like a child. Andrew, I have to know . . . ' But she too glanced at Betty and stopped.

'Come back to our room. We'll discuss it there.'

Leah took his proffered arm and dismissed the maid, but her voice shook.

'Why don't you sit down?' Andrew suggested when they reached their room. He was in two minds how much he ought to tell her about his transaction with Ward. At very least, he ought to set her mind at rest as far as Mr Barrowcliff was concerned.

Leah remained standing. She fumbled with the ribbons of her hat, her eyes scanning his face, as if she was trying to find the answer to a question he could not understand.

'What did Mr Barrowcliff want?'

Andrew explained briefly. He had expected Leah to be visibly relieved, but as she removed her hat, it concealed her face momentarily.

'Don't think I'm not grateful to you for — for sparing us all the ordeal of a trial,' Leah said, setting down her hat. 'But I must know what happened afterwards?'

'Afterwards?'

Andrew's gaze fell instinctively on the scattering of ash that had once been Ward's letter. Leah's restraint sent a chill to his heart. He realised that he had hoped that by burning the letter, he could atone for his mistakes. He saw now that the rift between them was wider than he had thought.

'I saw Mr Barrowcliff leaving from the window and when you didn't come back, I sent Betty to make enquiries. The landlord told her you'd asked the way to the Crown.' Her voice dropped even lower. 'I know who you went to see there.'

'Oh.' So much for keeping his

meeting with Ward a secret.

'You — you didn't challenge him to — to — '

'Challenge him? No, Leah, I assure you, the thought never crossed my mind.' Gently he took hold of her hands. 'I only wanted to tell him that there would be no prosecution against him and offered to lend him some money until he is on a more even keel. That's all, I swear.'

He saw the wonder in Leah's eyes. An incredulous smile spread across her face. Then she shook her head.

'You'll never get your money back,' she said.

'It's a risk I'm willing to take, if you will only forgive me for betraying your trust.'

'Oh, Andrew,' she murmured reproachfully, 'do you really need to ask that? Of course I forgive you.'

'You have my word as a gentleman,' Andrew said, returning her smile. 'And you must swear not to keep so many secrets or to protect any more fugitives from justice.'

Leah laughed out loud.

'I love you, Andrew Melbury,' she said, twining her arms round his neck and rising on tiptoe to tilt her mouth towards his. 'Now kiss me before I change my mind.'

THE END